GWENDOLINE

A
STORY
OF
LOVE
AND
TRAGEDY

JEREMY BENDING

CRANTHORPE
— MILLNER —
PUBLISHERS

First published by Cranthorpe Millner Publishers (2024)

ISBN 978-1-80378-189-1 (Paperback)

www.cranthorpemillner.com

Cranthorpe Millner Publishers

Printed and bound by CPI Group (UK) Ltd, Croydon, CR0 4YY

The front cover is an artistic impression depicting a scene from the Pevensey marshes in East Sussex. Gwendoline was to spend some of the happiest days of her life exploring the marshes during the idyllic summer of 1943, when in WW2 she and Roy were evacuated to the small village of Hooe, which sits on the edge of the marshes.

OTHER BOOKS BY JEREMY BENDING

A Listening Doctor

In the Shadows of the Birch Trees

If You Don't Know...

Impulses

In memory of
Gwendoline

29th June 1911 – 4th April 1974

Gone, but not forgotten.

April is the cruellest month, breeding
Lilacs out of the dead land, mixing
Memory and desire, stirring
Dull roots with spring rain.

T.S. Eliot.
The Waste Land. 1. The Burial of the Dead, 1922.
Selected Poems. Faber & Faber, 1954.

This book is a work of fiction. Although the story it tells is based on some real lives, the interpretation of those lives is mine alone. When I was not there to know the feelings of the people contained in the story, their hopes and fears, aspirations and regrets, these have arisen by necessity from my own imagination. If I may have imagined incorrectly in places, then those errors, while well-intentioned, are also mine alone; and a necessary step in telling the story that I knew should be told.

JB.

CHAPTER 1

The flat above Freeman, Hardy & Willis, the shoe shop on Western Road, Brighton, was the first home Gwen remembered as a young girl. Her father, Sidney Oddy, was described on his marriage certificate as a "cobbler". He had indeed started out as a shoemaker, but by the time Gwen was born, her father had been promoted to be the manager of the shop above which he and his wife Annie and their eleven children lived. The company, which had been founded in 1875, was proud to declare that it provided "shoes for all the family". In the case of Sidney's large family, this was no mean undertaking, and a considerable perk of his employment with the firm in the early part of the twentieth century. New shoes as and when required were provided free and "on the house" to all children of management employees of the company.

Gwen was one of the youngest of the children in the Oddy family. She'd had five brothers and five sisters, in addition to the sixth sister, Cissie, who had burnt to death as a young girl. Still in her night dress, she had been ironing clothes with an old smoothing iron that was being heated on the hob of burning coals next to the ironing board. A spark from the coals caught her night dress on fire and she burnt to death there in the living room. Her screams were horrendous for all the family to hear. Her mother Annie rushed into the room to find her daughter writhing in pain on the floor, her nightdress and her pretty long fair hair set alight in flames. Annie screamed out to Sidney for help and he and Annie dashed backwards and forwards with bowls of water from the kitchen sink to throw over Cissie. But they were unable to save their daughter, who died in her sobbing mother's arms in a very short time.

Gwen had been too young to remember the incident, but the horror of the story she was later told of her older sister's death was to haunt her for the rest of her life. This was a tragedy that had affected them all but was apparently accepted with more grit and determination by the close-knit family than would have been the case a century later. Both Gwen's parents had strongly held religious beliefs – they were committed members of the Congregational Church – and in the years to come explained to their other children that they'd had to accept their loss of Cissie as "God's Will". It was true that many children died in childhood in those days, particularly from infectious diseases and malnutrition, and this was one of the reasons that couples like Sidney and Annie had large families in the first place, as an insurance against life's cruel depredations. But this can't have made the death of Cissie any less terrible for her parents to bear.

When Gwen was about ten years old, her father was moved with his family to manage the Freeman, Hardy & Willis shop twenty miles east along the Sussex coast in Bexhill-on-Sea. This was hardly a promotion – being transferred from the large town of Brighton to its smaller neighbour, however pleasant and indeed rather genteel the new town might have been considered. The fact of the matter was that Sidney knew his transfer to the smaller branch would reduce his salary and affect the size of the pension he was to receive when he retired in only a few years' time. That was why the company had arranged to downgrade his position and its lower pensionable status. He was aware that the company had employed such a strategy with the managers of other branches who Sidney was in contact with. But he never sought to complain and never mentioned his insight into why his transfer was being made, not even to his wife Annie.

At the age of eleven, in 1922, Gwen went on to the secondary school on the Bexhill Downs. Shortly after this, the County School for Boys and Girls, which was later to become the Bexhill Grammar School, was opened half a mile up the road from her secondary school. But entry to the new school was by an academic examination. Gwen could not remember whether it had ever been suggested that her name should be put forward to transfer to this new school, or indeed whether she had actually taken the exam. It may have been that, being from such a large family of children whose parents, loving and caring though they were, were not from an academic background, the possibility of Gwen sitting an examination to gain entrance to the new

County School had not even been considered.

In spite of spending all of her time in the less scholarly secondary school, whether by design or default, Gwen proved herself as intellectually quite bright. She was certainly outwardly thinking enough to have aspirations to become something more than a secretary or housewife, which was the path of so many young women in that era, whether they liked it or not. She decided at a young age that she wanted to train to be a nurse, but at that time never had the courage to raise this possibility with her parents, who she feared would not approve of the idea.

CHAPTER 2

One evening in 1925 Gwen was sitting at the table in the living room doing her homework. Her father had finished his supper and was standing next to the fire with his waistcoat unbuttoned, lighting his pipe, his tie discarded and his shirt sleeves rolled up to his elbows after work. He coughed loudly to catch her attention, and Gwen looked up from her school books.

'So, my girl. You're fourteen at the end of June. What do you want to do with your life after you've left school in July?'

This was the moment that Gwen had been prepared for. She had known this question would arise sometime soon; now was the time for her to tell her father what was in her heart.

'I don't want to leave school, Father. I want to continue with my studies.'

'You're thinking of secretarial college then?' her father asked.

'No, Father. I don't want to become a secretary like a lot of the girls I know do. And I have no intention of becoming a housewife either, come to that!'

'Well, I can't think what else you might be wanting for yourself. Being a housewife has been a very satisfactory life for your mother. You're not getting ideas above your station, I hope?' her father challenged her, making clear his disapproval.

'No, Father. I want to train to be a nurse.'

'A nurse! That's a job only fit for "gentlewomen" to pursue. Either that, or it's the resort of "fallen" women, so they tell me! And you're not in either of those brackets, at least not in my house, and I forbid you ever taking up such an inappropriate occupation!'

Her father hit his pipe hard against the side of the grate, emptying the tobacco he had just spent some time packing into the pipe's bulb out into the fire in his anger at his daughter's stated intentions. Her mother stood at the open kitchen door, anxiously wiping a cup with a tea towel as she listened nervously to the exchange that had just taken place. But she kept quiet and said nothing in support of Gwen's wishes, evidently agreeing with her husband about the matter.

So, as fate would have it, Gwen had to wait until she was legally old enough to make her own decisions before she was able to leave home to enrol as a student nurse in London. In those days no sane young woman would run away from their home and parents and risk ending up in poverty, or worse. And, in any case, Gwen was a dutiful daughter who loved her parents. In spite of her father's unreasonable intransigence regarding her career aspirations, she did not want to leave home in anger, perhaps never to have contact with her family again. So she continued to bite her tongue, from then on not discussing the subject again with her mother or her father.

When she did leave the Downs secondary school that summer, she got herself a job in the haberdashery shop Greens on Devonshire Road. She loved it there; it was like a magic cave, with swatches of material and velvet curtains in all shades hanging down the walls, and drawers full of reels of cotton and buttons on cards. She was mesmerised at first by the cash carrier, which fired a metal canister pneumatically around the ceiling from the counter with money to the cashier in her cubicle, and a receipt and change from her back to the counter. The manageress was a kind woman who looked after Gwen and the other girls in the shop and treated them well, as long as they behaved themselves. And Gwen made a number of good friends while working there. The money she earned was not bad, although every Thursday when she received her weekly wage as cash in a brown envelope, she passed all of it on to her mother when she got home the same evening, to help with the family's expenses. Her mother would sometimes give her a sixpence back if Gwen asked if she could have something to spend on herself, such as a trip to the cinema with her friends at the weekend.

But Gwen never lost sight of her determination to become a nurse. She would avidly read any book or magazine with a nurse in the story and also made sure she got to see all the films about hospital life that were being shown at the Curzon cinema. In the September after she left school, she enrolled at night school and spent her evenings studying hard. She didn't tell her mother and father what she was studying for and why, and by that time they seemed to have lost interest in what she was doing in any case. Three years later, Gwen passed all her matriculation exams with adequate marks.

CHAPTER 3

Every Sunday Gwen would go to the Congregational church in Bexhill with her family for the morning service and, very often, back in the evening for the evening service as well. The morning service was generally very popular, with frequently as many as a hundred people in the congregation. As she grew up, what she came to like about the denomination was that it was a liberal church that encouraged free thinking. Indeed, there were quite a few liberal-minded politicians and other eminent members of society who had been brought up in the church in their early days. Each local church was allowed to run itself democratically by the members, rather than by diktats from bishops or popes above them, and encouraged to engage with the up-to-date life around them. In this and other respects, it was quite different from the Baptists, strict or otherwise, and the Methodists, both of whom frowned on many aspects of "normal" modern life at the beginning of the twentieth century.

Gwen was looking forward to the Halloween night party,

which was being held at the Territorial Army hall next to her old school on Thursday. Luckily, it was half term for her college, which meant that she would not have to miss her evening class on that day that week. When she arrived, with her younger brother Stuart to chaperone her, the partygoers were already having a good time. The hall was decked out with witches on broomsticks hanging from the ceiling and huge pumpkins that sat on every window sill, their eyes and mouths carved out, with gaping, jagged teeth and sinister grins, and lit up by tea light candles burning inside them. Her parents hadn't been interested in coming with them, but people of all ages were there, including entire families. A lot of those on the dance floor were older people, but Gwen was relieved to see that there were a good number of young people her age as well. As usual for those days, women considerably outnumbered men, especially younger men, who were often working away from home or in the forces.

One young man she recognised immediately was Roy Baines, who was standing by his own at the edge of the hall. He was the brother of her friend Muriel. He was a softly spoken, rather shy young man, tall and thin with his black hair neatly parted to one side. She chatted to him quite often in the church vestibule at the end of services or at meetings in the church hall. She had already learnt he was quite a serious young fellow, but an interesting one once you got to know him and not as silly as many of the young men of his age. Gwen had got to like him and was pleased when he looked up and gave her a wave from the other side of the hall as she walked in.

Roy appeared in front of her after about fifteen minutes. 'Would you like to dance, Gwen?'

Gwen was a pretty girl, with her hair tied up in a bun behind her head, and it was perhaps surprising that other men had not approached her to dance already. She didn't speak, but stood up and smiled at Roy in agreement, her head on one side. He reached out and took her right hand, placing his right arm around her waist as they stepped out onto the dance floor together. They did not have the luxury of a live band to dance to, but one of the men was in charge of a very good phonograph on the stage that made an adequate alternative. Gwen was enjoying herself and danced with Roy a number of times.

At the end of the evening, her brother Stuart seemed to have disappeared, but Roy offered to walk her home. They walked slowly, talking and listening to each other, sharing what had been happening to them recently. Roy started to tell Gwen about the building works his father's firm was involved in along the coast. He was clearly very excited about whatever this was, but did not go into the detail of what was involved, or its purpose.

'It's a state secret, really. I can't tell you mo...more. Please don't repeat any of this to anybody else, Gwen,' he added.

She had noticed before that Roy had a slight stammer, just occasionally, especially when he was excited.

'That's exciting, Roy. And, don't worry, I won't discuss this with a soul!' Gwen said with a little laugh, still completely unsure what it was he had been trying to tell her. She didn't want him to think she was mocking him.

As they reached her house, he took her hand. 'I've had a lovely evening. I say, Gwen, I don't sup...suppose you'd like to come with me to the Curzon sometime? I happened to notice in *The Observer* that there are a number of good films being shown over the next few weeks.'

'That would be lovely, Roy. Thank you for inviting me. I'll let you choose the film.' She stood on her tip toes and kissed him on the cheek. She waved goodbye as she let herself into her parents' house.

CHAPTER 4

One Friday night, the week after her twenty-first birthday, and after both her parents had gone to bed, Gwen reached down the suitcase from the top of the wardrobe in her bedroom. She began to pack it quietly – so as not to disturb her parents and her brothers and sisters who were still living at home – with the clothes and essential items she had been collecting together over the last few days. She had written to her aunt Hettie in Streatham – who was actually her mother's cousin – asking if she could come to stay with her for a while whilst she was applying for nurse training school. She told Hettie that she would be able to arrange her own accommodation as soon as she had been accepted. She had also explained in the letter that her parents had not approved of the idea of her training to become a nurse, but that she was dead set on it and desperately wanted to pursue a career in nursing. For this reason, she wrote to Hettie, she would very much appreciate it if she did not mention her plan to her mother or father at the moment.

She had received an enthusiastic and supportive letter from Hettie that morning, telling her that she and her husband would be very happy to accommodate Gwen for a while and promising not to tell her parents what she was planning until she was ready to do so herself.

So at four thirty the next morning, before even her mother had woken up, Gwen let herself out of the front door of the house with her suitcase and made her way to the Central station to catch the first train from Bexhill to Croydon. She left a note for her mother on the kitchen table, telling her she loved her and that she would be in touch within a few weeks.

Gwen was excited about the life ahead of her. The only regret she had was that she would be leaving Roy behind. By then they had become a couple and she knew this would only be a temporary separation. Roy had promised to come and visit her in Streatham as often as he could.

CHAPTER 5

In September 1932, aged twenty-one, Gwen entered nurse training school. She was the oldest girl in her year because she had not gone into nursing straight after leaving school, which was the case for the rest of her class. She had applied to and been accepted by St James' Hospital in Balham, South London. She hadn't known where to apply to and had picked St James' mainly because its entry qualifications were less rigorous and also because it was not far from her aunt Hettie's house in Streatham. She had been nervous about visiting the centre of London – she still was – but had also assumed that the most prestigious teaching hospitals in the centre of the capital would be unlikely to take her on.

But St James' Balham was a more ambitious place than she had anticipated. It was a large and busy hospital in a densely populated area of South London – a hospital of nearly nine hundred beds, planned to serve every need of the local population. The hospital board had decreed that no case should ever be refused, as a result of which the hospital received the whole spectrum of emergency and routine medical and surgical conditions. The hospital had come to acquire quite an eminent reputation since the Great War, not least in the surgical disciplines.

The School of Nursing was a popular place to train and took in a hundred and twenty student nurses every year to its three-year State Registered Nurse training course. During the 1920s, a new nurses' home had been built, accommodating a hundred and fifty-five members of staff, with another block for the nurses' home having been added three years later. Almost all of the nurses lived in the nurses' home, given the fact that it was next door to the hospital and convenient for the long hours they all had to work. Gwen moved in there at the start of her first term, thanking her aunt Hettie for having been so kind to her, so that she could now be independent and close to her place of work.

Her nursing training was very much centred on learning to care for the sick patient, although inevitably parts of the course included the teaching of basic anatomy and physiology. Gwen would never forget one summer afternoon when nursing tutor Margaret Young gave her group of student nurses an outdoor anatomy class on the terraced area of the roof of St James', using a full-size human skeleton hanging by its skull from a metal stand to illustrate the subject. The arms of the skeleton would sway backwards and forwards in the breeze from time to time, as if it was coming back to life once more in a *Danse Macabre*, now that it had been let out of its cupboard. Gwen and her student nursing colleagues could not resist giggling throughout the whole of the class as the skeleton jigged about behind the nursing tutor's back.

*

After completing her training and passing all her exams to become a State Registered Nurse, in 1935 Gwen obtained a post as a staff nurse in the casualty department of St. James'. This was a busy job, the arrival of accidents and emergencies never ceasing, twenty-four hours a day, in this populated area of South London.

One evening, she was on duty with another staff nurse colleague when the doors swung open and ambulance men started to bring in patients on stretchers from the row of ambulances that were drawing up outside, their blue lights flashing. The casualty department sister had gone off duty only fifteen minutes before. Gwen realised at once that this was some sort of general emergency, not just the arrival of one or two patients from a road accident or from home because of any other medical or surgical emergency.

Gwen stood at the door, rapidly assessing each patient and directing each stretcher case to the minor, major or critical beds in the department that were ready to accept newcomers. She had already picked up the phone and asked the switchboard to Tannoy all medical and surgical doctors in the hospital to report to casualty immediately. Her other staff nurse colleague was busy allocating other nurses and nursing auxiliaries to each available cubicle. She could see that all of the men being brought in – they appeared to be all men – were dressed in rags, malnourished and even emaciated. Their boots were dirty and worn down, their feet blistered and bleeding. Even in this area of South London, where there was so much poverty, she had not seen patients in this number who looked so impoverished. Not in one large group, in any case.

'What's going on, Bert?' she asked the next ambulance worker who had just brought a patient in. She recognised him from his frequent visits to the department. He was one of the ambulance crew based at the Balham ambulance station and St James' was therefore his most frequent port of call.

'It's the Jarrow boys,' Bert replied. 'They're being sent in to us from all over London – Edgware and Marble Arch and Westminster – in their scores.'

'What's this all about?' Gwen asked.

'Haven't you read the papers, love?' Bert replied. 'These poor boys are just a few of the thousands of bastards who have walked all the way from Jarrow in the north east of England to protest about the closure of the shipyard there and the poverty and unemployment they and their families live in.'

Gwen was astonished. It was a fact: her job was so busy that she very rarely had the time to listen to the wireless, let alone read a newspaper and know what was going on in the world outside her small island here at St James'. The department was by this

18

time being invaded by teams of doctors – medical and surgical – who had responded to her emergency call on the Tannoy, assessing each patient in the department as they went around.

After about an hour, the wave of emergencies had started to die down. Her staff nurse colleague swapped places with her at the entrance door, and Gwen started to walk around the cubicles, which were all full, with some trolleys still in the corridors, in spite of the fact that a number of patients had already been taken off to the surgical wards or even to theatre to be operated on for their broken limbs or other urgent surgical issue. She was giving reassurance to the patients, as well as to her more junior nursing colleagues and student nurses, who, like her, had never had to deal with an emergency anything like this before.

At that moment she felt like her heroine, Florence Nightingale, at the battle of Crimea. Very quickly, she was able to see that the men that had been admitted to the department were not truly "emergencies", in the strict definition of the word. They had bleeding blisters on their feet and sores elsewhere on their bodies, and most of them had collapsed with exhaustion onto the road as they reached London, their final destination, sometimes sustaining bony injuries as they did so. But all of them were so generally malnourished and emaciated as to come into the category of "chronic disease" patients. They had not been brutally injured by amputation or internal wounds from gunfire and ordnance, like the soldiers of the Crimean war. But they were starving and emotionally damaged by the life of poverty and depredation that they, their women and their children had had to endure. Either way, they had collapsed on the road and had been brought in by ambulance.

'Are you comfortable, sir?' Gwen asked the next patient she came to. She always spoke with respect to all her patients, whatever their social status, age or other category.

'Ahm alreet, bonnie lass,' he replied. Gwen was bemused for a moment by the man's reply in the vernacular.

'Where are you from, my dear?' she asked him.

'Ahm frae Jarrow, bonnie lass. Ahm a Geordie,' was the reply.

'Tell me about what has been happening,' Gwen asked, as she held the man's hand, sitting on the chair next to his stretcher.

The man told his story. He was a member of the Jarrow marchers, and had been walking on the road since the fifth of October to protest against the closure of the Palmers shipyard and the blocking of a proposed steelworks in Jarrow, in North East England. He began to tell Gwen in his foreign dialect about the poverty and unemployment that had existed for years in his part of the country. The closure of the one important source of work for men, and the disappointment about the alternative employment that might have replaced it, had been just too much for them all to bear. Thousands of men had marched from Jarrow to London to protest against their fate. Many of them had collapsed along the way. The rest had finally reached Westminster to present their petition to Parliament, only for some of them to collapse in the city having done so. Most of these casualties had been diverted to St James' in Balham to take them out of the spotlight of the capital. The government of the day was clearly embarrassed about the bad publicity this event was causing them.

'I left wor lass and eight bairns to come here,' the man said. 'Na ta say the four bairns who have left us already,' he concluded sadly.

Gwen did not get back to the nurses' home until about midday the next day, after she had done her very best to see to it that all of the Jarrow marchers had been properly looked after. The whole experience had left a big mark on her. She had been given an insight into the depth of poverty and injustice that existed in other parts of the country to a degree that was outside her own experience. She now, if never before, realised at last what nursing should be all about. After a night's sleep, she went in the next day, on her day off, to volunteer her help on one of the general wards to look after all the poor men who required nursing.

CHAPTER 6

Following her baptism in the casualty department, Gwen applied for a post as a staff nurse in the surgical department at St James'. She had obtained an enormous amount of experience in the casualty department already but was determined to get as much knowledge in all the specialities of nursing as she could. Her request for a transfer was accepted at once, and she started work in St James' operating theatres the next month.

The resident surgeon was a Mr Norman Tanner, who had worked in several London County Council Hospitals before being appointed as Senior Resident Surgeon to St James' Hospital in Balham. He was a quiet man, the antithesis of a self-promoter, unlike his other surgical colleagues, especially those in the more prestigious Central London teaching hospitals. In spite of all this, although Gwen did not know it at the time, he was to become one of the doyens of British and international general surgery, putting St James' Hospital on the map as a consequence.

One evening, Gwen was tidying up the theatre after the

afternoon operating session had finished, when a patient was brought in as an emergency. He was a twenty-five-year-old soldier who had been admitted to the acute bay of the casualty department. He had complained of sudden severe abdominal pain and by the time he reached St James', his condition was critical. He was barely conscious, pale and sweaty, with a scarcely recordable blood pressure. Mr Tanner was summoned urgently via the hospital Tannoy. He took only seconds to assess the patient and then had him wheeled straight round to the operating theatre. Sister Jones had already gone off duty. Gwen was the only nurse still in theatre, working on a late shift until the night staff came on. She took one look at the patient and started to open the emergency packs.

'Scrub up, staff nurse, there's no time to lose!' Mr Tanner directed her firmly but politely as he hurried into the theatre, the anaesthetist, Dr Scott, following close behind him. He opened the lever taps on the sink with his elbows and started soaping up immediately. Gwen stood at the sink next to him, scrubbing up herself. Once they had both done so, Gwen opened a sterile gown pack and handed it to the surgeon, tying the straps for him behind his back as he stood with his elbows bent, his clean hands raised in the air, before he pulled on the sterile gloves from a pack on the counter Gwen had also prepared for him. She opened a gown pack and gloves for herself, put these on and barely had time to join Mr Tanner on the opposite side of the table before he commenced operating. He had already cleansed the man's skin with iodine solution and draped the sterile green sheets over his abdomen. He was holding out his hand to her to receive the scalpel she passed to him.

Gwen had never seen Mr Tanner – or any other surgeon, come to that – work so fast. But not only was he quick, he was totally calm and controlled in his every move. Having opened the abdomen with his scalpel, he soon had the stomach and duodenum exposed and was methodically locating and clamping each artery in the order that he needed to isolate them. This was not an easy matter: the man's abdominal cavity was filled with arterial blood that was gushing up at him without ceasing, like a mill pond below a stream in torrent. Gwen stood with the sucker in her hand, struggling to aspirate as much of the blood as she could without getting in the way of Mr Tanner's progress. She could hardly keep up with him, but she knew she had to keep calm and concentrate fully.

She saw sweat pouring off Dr Scott's face out of the corner of her eye. He was struggling to cannulate collapsed veins in the man's neck in an attempt to gain extra access to fill the patient's circulation with universal donor blood. Every few seconds Mr Tanner would indicate the next suture to be cut, holding it up with the end of his forceps, and each time Gwen would lean forward into the abdomen with her scissors and cut the suture as quickly but as precisely as she could. Eventually, the bleeding was controlled and Mr Tanner swabbed out the remaining blood as she handed clean swabs on forceps to him one by one. She could see the colour of the patient's skin pinking up a little and she sensed that the anaesthetist was starting to relax. She leant across the patient and gently wiped the sweat off Mr Tanner's brow with a clean cloth. As soon as she had done so, it occurred to her that perhaps she should have asked his permission first. But before she could worry about that, Tanner's eyes looked across at her over his surgical mask. 'Thank you, nurse,' was all he said.

Once Mr Tanner had excised the bleeding duodenal ulcer and anastomosed the gut ends, he closed the abdomen with different layers of precise sutures. The surgery had been completed successfully and the anaesthetist was arranging with the porters to transfer the patient back to the recovery room. Gwen cleared away the instruments, cleaned up the table and joined Mr Tanner at the sinks, where they stood scrubbing down together.

'Where did you train, staff nurse?' he asked her as she unwound his gown for him and took it off him.

'Here at St James', sir,' she replied.

'Very good,' Tanner said. 'Thank you,' was all he added before he turned and left the theatre. Gwen felt elated that she had been able to help such an expert surgeon in what had been a serious emergency. She knew he had saved the man's life, and she hoped that her part in the operation had been satisfactory. She turned her attention to making the operating theatre ready for the next patient that might require it.

CHAPTER 7

Two days later, Gwen was leaving for duty on another late shift, having completed an early shift the day before. On her way out, she looked into the office in the nurses' home entrance where the pigeon holes were to see if she had received any post. She was hoping for a letter from Roy. Instead, what she found appeared to be an official-looking hospital letter addressed to her by typewriter. She sat down on a chair in the office and opened the letter.

"Dear Miss Oddy,

I am pleased to inform you that you have been appointed to the post of Theatre Sister here at St James'. You have been allocated to work principally with Mr Tanner, although you will of course assist the other surgeons out of hours and during emergencies, should the need arise.

May I be the first to congratulate you on this promotion, which I have no doubt you have earned. You will be commencing this post from the first of next month. I trust this is acceptable to you. You will be receiving a separate formal letter of appointment setting out your terms and conditions of service from the staffing department shortly. Will you please call into the sewing room to be measured for your sister's uniforms. I look forward to meeting up with you in the sisters' dining room in due course.

With kind regards,
Mrs Joan Exley, SRN, Matron."

Gwen sat for a few minutes taking in the news. She couldn't believe it was true. She had not even put in an application for promotion – she would have considered herself too junior in experience, if not in years, to do so this soon after having qualified – let alone undergone a formal interview for the post. Nevertheless, she was thrilled and excited by the letter and felt as if a great honour and challenge had been placed on her. She went off to work to start her next shift feeling elated, but did not mention the letter to any of the other nurses she was working with that afternoon. As soon as she got off for her break that evening, she sat down and wrote a hurried note with the good news to Roy.

"Darling, that's wonderful news!" she read in the letter from him that arrived in the return post. She had torn it open immediately. "You must be very excited. I'm so proud of you. With all my love, yours as ever, Roy."

There was a P.S. at the bottom: "P.S. I know without you

mentioning it that this will mean quite a significant pay rise. That will come in very handy! I was about to write and tell you that I have come by a nice little house that should suit us fine on Glenthorn Road. There's a bit of work that needs doing first, but this should be finished within a few months. What do you think?"

Gwen sat down quickly, tears of joy streaming down her face. She knew the P.S. meant he was asking her to marry him. She had expected he was going to pop the question soon, but now that it had happened, at the same time as her unexpected promotion, she could not believe it. She was so happy. She sent him a telegram that morning. It read: "Yes, please. I love you. G xxx."

CHAPTER 8

It did not take Gwen long to get into the swing of things in her new position as Sister in charge of one of the operating theatres at St James'. In fact, she found it quite easy to take the lead and was relieved to find that the other nurses and operating department assistants now under her command made it easy for her to grow into her new role. Although nobody was so forward as to say so, they seemed to tacitly acknowledge that they thought she knew what she was doing and were enthusiastic to work in her team with her as their new leader.

Mr Tanner had three scheduled operating sessions a week for non-urgent, booked cases in addition to the emergency sessions that he would undertake at any time of the day or night, seven days a week. Gwen didn't know how he kept it up, working at such intensity. But her loyalty to him meant that she was determined to make herself available, as his nominated theatre sister, to be the one to assist him at every operating session he undertook. She insisted to the nurses on her team that they

29

should contact the switchboard operator to call her whenever Mr Tanner was being called in for an emergency, whatever time of the day or night that was. This meant that, following her promotion to the role, she got precious little time off herself. Quite often, Roy would drive up to see her at a weekend and find himself waiting alone in her room in the sisters' wing of the nurses' home while she assisted Mr Tanner in theatre with an emergency operation they had been called in for. He would sit reading a book he had brought with him to cover this eventuality. He didn't seem to mind. He told her he was proud of what she was doing.

One Wednesday at the end of his planned morning operating session, Mr Tanner sat in the surgeon's room having a cup of coffee with Gwen before he started his afternoon clinic. He had got into the habit of inviting her to join him at the end of the list.

'I apologise if you have noticed me asking the same question twice on occasion, Sister Oddy.' He was at all times correct enough to use her surname, but he always preceded it by "Sister".

'I haven't noticed, sir,' Gwen replied, a little flustered by what he might be trying to tell her.

'The fact is, I'm rather deaf. I thought you must have noticed, and I wanted to explain if you had.'

Gwen did not know what to say. The truth was that she hadn't noticed, but now he mentioned it, she could think of a number of occasions when he had repeated a question to her. She had assumed at the time that this was just due to the fact that he had been concentrating hard on his work, his mind glued on the operation in progress.

Mr Tanner went on to explain to her that he had a form of congenital deafness – he had been born with it.

'That is the reason I was turned down for the armed services,' he explained, almost apologetically. 'They wouldn't have me because of my deafness.'

'Well, I would not have known about your hearing problem if you hadn't told me, sir. It doesn't affect your ability as a surgeon. I think you do a really grand job.' She always spoke to Mr Tanner with correctness herself, never wanting to sound familiar, but they had reached the stage in their professional work together when she felt she could speak truthfully to him without being sycophantic. In fact, as she considered what she had just said to him now, she realised it was important that she should openly declare her support for what he was doing, not just by her silent respect. Indeed, as his nominated theatre sister, she considered she now had a responsibility to encourage him in his work and to let him know she admired him for it. Mr Tanner said nothing in reply, but beamed broadly at her before changing the subject. From then on, their working relationship and respect for each other became well and truly cemented.

So now they were an established team. This meant that, in the years before the Second World War, with Gwen to support him, Tanner worked through an epidemic of peptic ulceration during which his daily operating lists were astonishing. With no registrar assistant, he and Gwen as his theatre sister also shared the post-operative care of the patients. Very early every morning, before commencing that day's operating list, she would do a round of all the post-operative patients under his care, to ensure that they were progressing well, and report back to Mr Tanner before he started operating. He came to trust her judgement completely and would always go and see any patient immediately if she felt they were not doing well for any reason, sometimes having to take them back to theatre if that was the case. As a result, the team work he developed with her enabled him to free up extra time to concentrate on operating on many more patients – some of whom needed urgent surgery – than he would have been able to had he been working completely alone. Gwen knew that she would never have been given so much responsibility in any of the Central London hospitals, where surgeons would have teams of house surgeons and surgical registrars to assist in the day-to-day care of their patients.

During her time with Mr Tanner, the two of them together were able to care for an extraordinary number of patients needing urgent surgery. Mr Tanner kept detailed records of all the patients he had operated on and their outcome and survival figures. With time, he was able to publish his experience, which included reporting the outcome of 1,275 surgical procedures for duodenal and gastric ulcers with an overall mortality below 1.5 per cent, a low morbidity and excellent cure rates. He had encountered and developed a system for the management of massive gastro-duodenal bleeding from various causes in six hundred and fifty patients. He was an early proponent of operating for the excision of gastric carcinoma, which he undertook at the same time as selectively excising lymph node groups based on the same principles as those applied by Clifford Dukes to large bowel cancers.

Gwen had taken an immediate liking to Mr Tanner from the day she started working with him, respecting him as a person and as a surgeon, which was the reason that their teamwork flourished, based on mutual respect. Before long, his elegant, gentle technique had become well known outside the confines of St James' and was starting to be copied and safely performed elsewhere by surgeons of only average competence. The fact that Mr Tanner had become recognised as a master surgeon was illustrated by the fact that with time, he was allocated a surgical assistant by the hospital board to join him in his practice. A lengthy queue of hopeful applicants to be his assistants was soon established. Early on, nearly all of these were trainees from the Commonwealth, since British surgical registrars were initially misguidedly reluctant to risk enlisting with a surgeon who practised outside the centre of London as their exemplar. But Gwen was proud to be working with the man, and in return he still relied on her just as much as his principal trusted assistant, in spite of the trainee surgical registrars who were now being appointed to his service.

After the Second World War, it became the custom for surgeons to visit each other and watch new and highly effective operations being performed by the surgeons who had developed them. They would turn up unannounced at St James' and be invited to scrub up to assist and learn the fine points of Tanner's technique. Scores of surgeons from many advanced and less advanced countries crowded into his makeshift operating theatre at St James' to watch him at work. They would take advice and inspiration from him and, in the years that followed, would be proud to declare to other surgeons, "I'm a Tanner trainee". So it was no surprise to Gwen to hear that, sometime after she had left his service, in 1945, he had been promoted to Consultant at St James', and in 1953, he was also invited to join the consultant staff of the Charing Cross Hospital in London.

But not all the surgeons she worked with were the same as Mr Tanner. She was by now running an operating theatre as a highly qualified professional senior sister, in which role she had also had to develop the ability to deal with the verbal tantrums of some of the other more *prima donna* surgeons. During their operating sessions she sometimes found herself being required to duck, along with the rest of her theatre team, the physical missiles that the surgeon may have chosen to hurl across the operating theatre. These quite often followed the verbal assaults that the man was also known to frequently let rip. These more unpleasant experiences only cemented her admiration for Norman Tanner as a special surgeon and a special person.

CHAPTER 9

The time came, however, when Gwen decided that she should move on from her post as operating theatre sister at St James', Balham. She had come to realise that she had literally become married to the job. The many hours a week without time off meant that she was seeing Roy less and less often than either of them wished for. She talked it over with Roy, and he agreed. She could see that he was, in fact, hugely relieved. As soon as she had made her decision, she told Mr Tanner about her intentions during their break for coffee following the next operating session they had together. He was a gentleman in his response, but not afraid to show his disappointment at losing her. He told her how valuable her work with him had been and how much he would miss working with her. He said that of course he would be very happy to give her a reference for any new job she wished to apply for and added that he would take her back at any time, should circumstances change, although they both knew that that was unlikely.

Having made the break from St James' theatres, Gwendoline decided on a career path that she hoped would be decidedly more peaceful. She applied to become a district nurse in the Streatham Common area of South London and was accepted immediately. She went back to live with her aunt Hettie and her husband, this time paying them rent from her earnings to lodge in a room in their family home on the north side of the Common. She would cycle round the schools of Streatham being responsible for the health and welfare of the school children. One of her most used implements in this role was her nit comb, which was in constant use for painstakingly combing out the head lice that inhabited the hair of large numbers of the children. It was true that, being no respecter of social class, head lice were rampant in children of the poor and well-off alike. But she soon found out that the job of a district nurse involved being needed to care for patients with many more serious health issues than head lice.

The district nurses in her district would congregate in the basement around a big table in the superintendent's office at eight o'clock every morning. The office was not far from her digs on the north side of the Common, but Gwen would take her bicycle with her so that she could leave from there to cover her visits for the rest of the day. When she first started, she was shadowed for a few days by a supervising district nurse and then expected to take on her own workload, which soon proved to be extremely heavy. After visiting homes all morning, she would come back to the office for lunch and spend the afternoon writing up her notes and sending messages to general practitioners (GPs) before starting her evening visits about five p.m. She would write her messages on headed notepaper in her precise and professional copperplate handwriting. At their early morning meetings, the district nurses would usually have time to discuss the sickest and most problematic patients they had seen the day before. The superintendent, in spite of her rather grand title, was an elderly retired hospital matron who was very supportive of all her district nurses' workloads and difficulties. Other than those daily meetings, Gwen's main professional contact was with the GPs whose patients she nursed, but whom she rarely got to see in person. Most of the time, she would communicate with a GP via written notes, although from time to time she would receive a telephone message from a GP via the superintendent's office.

Many of the older GPs, who had qualified before introduction of the developing district nursing service, would use her rarely. And when they did, they would usually only ask her to undertake something simple, such as to give an enema to one of their patients. They certainly were not aware of her previous training and experience, which also included her ability to act as a midwife and health visitor. She often felt frustrated that she was being seriously underutilised by those out-of-date practitioners. But she did not blame the individual GPs, who had not yet understood the potential benefit an experienced district nurse could provide for their patients and indeed themselves.

Much of the time Gwen would work alone all day, sustained by the overall good humour and appreciation of her patients and their families, with no other contact with another nursing or medical colleague. It was on those days that she missed the responsibility and teamwork she had become used to, working so closely with Mr Tanner at St James'. She was entirely competent to take on antenatal and postnatal work as well as diagnose and treat many ailments. The fact of the matter was that the majority of patients and their families who Gwen attended were too poor to be able to afford the fee for a GP's visit. Her services to them were free of charge, and for this reason if no other, they were dependent on her, expecting her to act as a substitute doctor. To the best of her ability, she endeavoured to cope with all these poor families largely on her own as much as she could, only calling for medical help in the most difficult cases, to prevent them having to incur a doctor's fee.

But with time, she came across some GPs, usually the younger ones, who viewed her work as an essential help, and after a while even came to view her as a staunch ally. Gwen was always very well dressed and professional, in her blue uniform and district nurse badge, even when she'd had to cycle to see a patient in the pouring rain. At those times she would throw her large black cape over herself, covering the handle bars and rest of her bike at the same time. Many GPs were struggling for enough work to make a living themselves, so there was competition from some with what the district nurses were doing, but this was usually good-humoured. The fact that the health visitors were employed by local government rather than by fundraising and subscription could also be a friction.

There had been a dramatic increase in district nurses during the inter-war years. By the time Gwen came to the role, there were already eight thousand district nurses in Great Britain. More than forty per cent of these were financially supported by the population they served, through fundraising by voluntarily run local associations. About half of the district nurses in the country were Queen's Nurses. These were nurses who had been specially trained at Queen Victoria's Jubilee Institute for Nurses, which had been founded by the late Queen in 1887. The Institute had centralised training for district nurses and had developed a reputation for high standards in district nursing. As a State Registered Nurse, Gwen had had to learn on the job and was initially often looked down on by the qualified Queen's Nurses. But almost all of these came to appreciate her when they learnt about her previous training and experience, not to mention her competence and devotion to her patients. Other than that, her work was inspected twice a year by the superintendents who were mostly concerned with maintaining standards and discipline rather than encouraging constructive interaction and further in-service training.

A large proportion of cases that district nurses cared for in the 1930s and 1940s were for respiratory diseases and childhood infections. Another important part of Gwen's job was to participate in the nationwide survey collecting the figures for maternity nursing and maternal mortality, as well as the nursing of patients with ante-natal and post-natal complications, notifiable diseases such as tuberculosis, puerperal fever, chicken pox and whooping cough. She was also deeply involved with public health concerns such as undernourishment and poor housing conditions, factors that were increasingly becoming recognised as underlying causes of otherwise preventable deaths and were therefore a primary concern to all district nurses, including herself.

It would break Gwen's heart to come across families that were so poor that they did not have enough money to feed their children properly. She would quite often enter households where the little ones were near starvation. On one occasion, when she asked a small girl quietly when she had last had a meal, the malnourished little girl looked up at her with a bemused face and said, 'Forgotten, miss.'

The mother and father in those families were usually painfully thin as well, using any money they had to buy food for the children but going hungry themselves. It also pained her to see the children walking around barefoot, not only indoors but around the streets, their parents too poor to buy new shoes after the last pair had fallen to pieces. She wished she could scoop all these children up and plonk them in her father's shop, to be measured for a brand new pair of shoes each, on the house of course.

Her off-duty consisted of one half-day per week and only occasional weekends, so most of the time Roy would drive up to be with her when he could. But her time was more fluid than it had been working in the operating theatres of St James'. At weekends particularly, she would only need to go out if called to a particular emergency, so she and Roy could spend much more time together. They spent the time excitedly planning their wedding and their lives together, and each time he came to visit, Roy brought her news on the progress of the work on the house on Glenthorn Road. Gwen could not wait to see it.

CHAPTER 10

One Sunday evening, before Roy left to drive back down to the south coast, they sat together talking about their career plans and how these could progress while at the same time working towards their marriage together.

'I've been meaning to tell you,' Roy said to her, 'I've changed my mind about staying with my father's building firm in the long term.' Gwen was surprised to hear this. Roy had never told her directly, but somehow she had assumed that this was what he wanted.

'Oh, I see,' Gwen replied. 'What is it you have in mind instead, Roy?'

'I'm not really sure, but I'm thinking over what my options are at the moment. It somehow seems all too easy just to go along the line that my parents and others have assumed would be my future. Look how determined you were to follow your own path in life, in spite of your father's opposition.'

Gwen might have replied that she did not have any

responsibility to her father's business, but she didn't.

'I understand, Roy. You know that whatever you decide to do, I shall be there to support you.'

'I know,' Roy said. 'And I also know what a lucky man I am to have you to love me.'

When she thought about it later, Gwen had been secretly a little disappointed when Roy told her he had decided against continuing to work with his father in the family building firm and that he was intent on forging a different career for himself. She wanted him to be happy with what he did in his life, but at the same time realised that his decision might lead to some uncertainty and delay for their plans together.

It was not because she wasn't keen on her future husband being a builder. In fact, she had very little knowledge about what Roy joining the company as a partner would have meant – she had no real idea about the details of what it was Roy's father did for a living. She certainly did not feel that having a husband as a builder might be climbing back down the social ladder herself. How could she? Her own father had been a simple shoemaker before he had made a success of that in his own way, which had led to his promotion in the business of Freeman, Hardy & Willis, so that he had risen to become one of the company's most valued managers.

*

A few months after Roy and Gwen had been "going out"

together, she was invited to have dinner at his parents' house on Wickham Avenue, on the "better" side of the town. She knocked quietly on the front door and stood waiting. The door was opened by Roy's mother, Emma Lydia. She was a tall, thin and rather regal woman with her long black dress and a black velvet choker with a pearl at the front of it around her long neck.

'Do come in, my dear. I'm pleased to meet you,' she said, shaking Gwen's hand and leading her into the large polished hall. 'Let me take your coat. Roy has told us all about you – in fact he never stops talking about you!' Gwen smiled sheepishly but was not sure whether this was a compliment or a sarcastic comment from Roy's mother. As the evening progressed, Roy's mother was friendly enough but did seem to Gwen to be somewhat aloof. She looked and acted not unlike Gwen imagined Queen Mary, the wife and Queen Consort of the present King George V, would – the lady of whom it was once said, "she was magnificent, humorous, worldly, in fact nearly sublime, though cold and hard". The more Gwen thought about it, the more she decided that Roy's mother did look exactly like the pictures she had seen of the Queen.

Emma Lydia led Gwen from the hall into a sitting room, where a large fire was alight. Standing in front of it was Roy's father, Frank Bausor Baines, dressed in a morning suit with a silk waistcoat, from which was hanging a gold watch chain. He was a short man of Edwardian appearance, with a bald head circled by white hair around the neckline and a white moustache. He came forward to shake Gwen's hand, almost formally, before turning towards a drinks cabinet in the corner of the room.

'Can I get you a glass of sherry, Gwendoline?' he asked, turning to her rather ceremoniously, beckoning her to take a chair in front of the fire.

'Thank you, Mr Baines,' she replied as she sat down. 'That would be nice.'

She had been on the point of calling him "sir" before choosing the less formal "Mr", which she had then decided would be more appropriate. She had the immediate feeling, however, that he was a man who was very used to being referred to as "sir". Mr Baines sat in the chair opposite her in front of the fire and talked to her about his recent business successes and his standing in the town, politically and socially, but at no time did he ask her any questions about herself or really expressed any interest in her. She was not a person who judged others, especially on the first time of meeting. But, in addition to being small in height, he immediately came across to her as rather pompous and full of his own importance.

As she sat there listening to him, she could not believe how different he was from his son Roy, the man she had fallen deeply in love with. At that moment, Roy came into the room, which saved any further embarrassment she might have been feeling, as he welcomed her and kissed her on the cheek. She started to relax.

As they sat down to dinner in the dining room, a maid appeared with the first-course dishes and Gwen couldn't help feeling that she was a little out of her social depth again. She had never been invited to a house with a maid before, even though this was not an uncommon occurrence in those days. Indeed, Gwen had a number of friends, including one of the girls she had first met in the haberdashery shop, who were now working as maids themselves. She already knew that Roy and his three sisters were keen on tennis and driving fast cars, another thing that made her sensitive about the gap in their social class.

Roy's father had already taken the initiative in the mealtime conversation and was now speaking at length about some Liberal politician he had recently had the pleasure of meeting. Gwen was not very familiar with political matters and hoped she would not be called upon to give her opinion. She sat opposite Mr Baines, looking over his shoulder to a picture hanging above the mantelpiece. It was a portrait of Roy's father wearing an ermine cloak with an ornate gold chain around his chest.

'I see you're looking at Pa's picture up there.' Roy had caught her eye. 'Did you know Father was the Mayor of Bexhill in 1926?'

She didn't know this – he had never told her! – but replied that she had "forgotten". She was not sure whether to be pleased or ashamed that Roy thought it mattered.

CHAPTER 11

Roy was well aware that it had always been assumed that he would take over the family building firm from his father when the time came – not least because he was his father's only son and brother to three sisters – but he had never really been all that keen on the idea himself. In spite of these family expectations, he was now determined to seek out a career elsewhere, as he had told Gwen. Gwen was doing really well in her chosen nursing profession, first as a theatre sister and now as a district nurse, and they both agreed that they did not want to rush into marriage for this reason, if no other. This decision therefore gave Roy time to decide what he really wanted to do with his life, and how he wanted to further his own career.

He applied through the Joint Matriculation Board to a further education college in Hastings, which gave him a wide range of subjects to choose from. He sat at home one evening reading through the college's brochure and the various curriculums on offer. Finally, he chose the electronics syllabus.

This was a subject he had always been interested in and one that he knew had good work prospects in the 1930s. He put in his application and was very soon accepted.

He started the course the following September. It would take him three years to finish it, but he and Gwen agreed that this would be time well spent as they both established their careers before they settled down together, wherever that might be. An important advantage of the course from Roy's point of view was that the majority of the taught part of the syllabus took place at the evening school. This meant that he could continue to work for – and be paid by – his father in the office of Strange & Sons Builders, even though he had decided that this was not his preferred career option in the long term. He had still not had the courage to break this information to his father.

Roy put his heart into being successful in his new course and found that he was enjoying the subject enormously. He had no doubt that it would lead to a good job at the end of it, wherever that might be. The time seemed to fly by, and he came out at the end of the course with a first-class pass mark, which pleased him greatly. Gwen was proud of him.

With his new certificate under his belt, Roy applied for a job with the electronics company Pye. He was called to an interview in London and offered a job by letter by the end of that week. The position he had been offered was in the Pye plant in Cambridge, not exactly near to his family home in East Sussex – although that didn't matter for now – but still rather a long way away from Gwen in Streatham. They discussed the situation together and decided he should go for it. The pay was really good and would help them with the money they were saving towards their future married life. When he had the chance to look at the timetables, he found that trains into London from Cambridge were very frequent and it would not take him long to get a bus from Liverpool Street station to visit Gwen at her digs in Streatham. He could see that the journey might not take him much longer than the drive up from the south coast he had got used to.

Once he and Gwen had decided he should go for the new job, he told his father that this post would be of help to him in the future if he remained with the firm. He still felt unable to tell his father directly that this might turn into a long-term career for him, which would mean him turning his back on his father's building business. He knew that his father would be devastated to learn that this might be the case.

William Pye had founded his company W.G. Pye & Co. Ltd in Cambridge in 1896. Pye had been the superintendent of the Cavendish Laboratory workshop and his electronics enterprise had been set up as a part-time business making scientific instruments. By the beginning of World War One in 1914, the company already had forty people manufacturing instruments for use in teaching and research. The war increased the demand for such instruments and the development of components provided the company the technical knowledge to lead it to build the first wireless receiver, which was to be used by the British Broadcasting Company.

Roy found himself part of a pioneering company at an exciting time for the development of electronics. He was based in the company premises in York Street, Cambridge, mainly on the design side. He found suitable digs with a room in a lady's house within walking distance of both his job and the railway station. He was working on developing an innovative new radio valve. A separate company had by this time also been established to build wireless components in the Cambridge Works at Church Path in Chesterton. By the time Roy arrived, William Pye had sold the company, now named Pye Radio Ltd, to a Mr C.O. Stanley, who started to set up a chain of small component manufacturing factories across East Anglia.

Stanley was fascinated by the new technology around television broadcasting and passed on his enthusiasm to Roy and the rest of his company. Together, they went on to build a high gain receiver that could pick up the BBC transmissions from Alexandra Palace. During Roy's time with the company, in 1937, a small television receiver was marketed by the company and had sold two thousand television sets at an average price of thirty-four pounds. With the outbreak of World War Two, the Pye receiver and one of the valves Roy had been working on was to become a key component of many military radar receivers. From then on, the company would go from strength to strength with its designs for other radio components required in the war effort. In the run up to all this, Roy's career in electronics was blossoming and his position in the company now secure. He and Gwen started to discuss the possibility that their life after their marriage might be based in Cambridge and that perhaps they should be looking for a house to settle down in in that city. That would mean abandoning their planned home on Glenthorn Road, Bexhill-on-Sea, which could be sold to help pay for a place in Cambridge.

*

On the thirteenth of February 1939, Roy received a telegram in Cambridge to tell him that his father Frank Bausor Baines had died suddenly at home on Wickham Avenue at the age of only sixty-three. His mother had found him dead, sitting in his favourite arm chair in his study. Their GP, Dr Winchester, thought that he had suffered a stroke, and "acute cerebral haemorrhage" was the cause of death that he put on Frank's death certificate. His father's gold fob watch had been found hanging on the dead man's waistcoat. It had apparently stopped at the exact time his father died, or so his mother later insisted. Roy travelled straight down to Bexhill to support his mother as soon as he received the telegram. He was very shocked and sad to learn the news about his father's sudden death himself. It had not been something he had been anticipating.

When he arrived at his parents' house on Wickham Avenue, Bexhill, he found his mother Emma surprisingly calm and collected. She had obviously been crying – he could see it from her red-rimmed eyes – but she clearly had already had time to decide that she did not want to be pitied as a newly widowed woman by the rest of her family. She was a proud and stoical woman. Her three daughters Marguerite, Muriel and Megan had already been clucking supportively around her. He found his mother on her own, sitting upright in the drawing room with no light on, even though it was dusk outside. He sat down beside his mother and took her hand.

'I'm so sorry, Mother,' he said.

'It's got to happen to us all, son,' she replied. 'It's just that it was all so sudden. An unwelcome surprise, to put it mildly.'

'I know,' Roy told her. 'You are being so brave.'

'Thank you, Roy,' she said, taking her lace handkerchief to her eyes for the first time since he had arrived. Roy thought about what else he should say.

'What about the company?' he asked finally. 'Who's going to look after that from now?'

His mother looked at him with a start. 'Why you, of course, Roy!' she cried. 'You know how it all works and the successful business your father has built up can't be allowed to wither on the vine. You have to keep it going in your father's memory. You'll do fine.'

Later that evening, after his mother had gone to bed and his three sisters were playing whist in the drawing room, Roy sat on the chair in the hall and rang Gwen. For the first time since hearing the news of his father's death, he gave in to emotion and shed some tears himself. At the other end of the line Gwen started crying herself. He knew she would. She was his sole supporter.

When they had both regained their composure, Roy told Gwen the response he had received from his mother following his question about the future of his father's company. There was a pause at the end of the line.

'You've got to take over, Roy. You have really no choice. At least, for the time being. You can't leave the company and your mother high and dry. It might only be for a short time. It will give your mother time to consider what she wants to do following the death of your father, and you can always resume your career in electronics with Pye if you still have that ambition. I'm sure they will understand and take you back without hesitation later, should that still be your wish. I'll resign from my job as a district nurse once you've got things sorted out down there. We'll get married and live at Glenthorn Road as soon as the future becomes clear.'

That last sentence persuaded Roy. That was what he wanted above all else.

CHAPTER 12

In early 1939, at the age of only twenty-six, Roy had therefore now found himself in charge of his father's company, running the building firm from its office at the end of Terminus Road, Bexhill-on-Sea. "Strange & Sons (Bexhill-on-Sea) Ltd, Builders & Sanitary Engineers", it read over the entrance. (Gwen never was sure where the inclusion of "Sanitary Engineers" came from in the title, she would joke to him.) The firm was a family-run building company that prided itself on individually built, quality homes.

Since Roy had taken charge, the company's azure blue headed writing paper now displayed the company title and at the top left-hand corner, the heading, "Directors: Frank Roy Baines (Roy) and Emma Lydia Baines" (Roy's mother who stayed on the paper long after Roy's father was dead). Following their marriage, the name "G.M. Baines" (Gwen) would be added to the list of directors, even though Gwen was only ever a director in name alone.

The firm had been founded by a Mr Strange in Tunbridge Wells in 1824. Roy's father, Frank Bausor Baines, had actually only started off as an office boy there but had gained respect and, by good fortune, had been appointed by Strange & Sons to manage a new branch in Bexhill when it was opened in 1910. However, with the sudden death of his father, Roy had not only inherited the company but found himself having to deal with considerable debts that his father had left behind upon his death. With hard work and application, Roy went about paying these off over time. In due course, he was also able to go on to buy out complete control of the firm from the Strange family, although the company continued to trade under their name.

Roy was a mild-mannered, polite and sensitive man. Whatever reservations he might have had at the beginning about entering the family firm, with time he became what was known in the trade as a "master" builder and an FIOB – Fellow of the Institute of Builders. He was, in other words, not someone who got his hands dirty, but definitely the person who ran the show and the manager of the company. In Roy's case, this meant that he was also a surveyor, architect and designer all rolled up into one. He prided himself in providing a high-quality, personalised service in the building, renovating and decorating of houses for all his customers. He was hardworking, principled and trusted, attributes that were greatly admired by his family and customers alike, but not something that was going to make him extraordinarily rich, which, as it was to turn out, it didn't. Apart from anything else, he was clearly too ethical to become a successfully rich businessman.

The office of Strange & Sons was situated above the showroom at the bottom of Terminus Road. The builders' yard was next door to the office. The showroom downstairs contained a pretty basic display of pictures of the firm's buildings past and present and of the buildings being planned in the future, all of which could be viewed through the shop window. The offices upstairs consisted of a number of rooms on the first floor of the building, the largest of which was Roy's office at the end of the corridor, with its director's desk and framed certificates on the wall. The corridors had dark-brown lino flooring and always smelt highly of polish. The other two or three rooms were occupied by Roy's secretary, Jean, and his assistant, Basil Chart.

The firm of Strange & Sons included many long-serving staff. Henry Dalloway was the senior foreman, running the yard with hard work, decency and utter commitment. Albert Smith, the chief lorry driver, was another, part of the bone marrow of the company. The master craftsmen included the carpenters ("chippies"), electricians ("sparks"), plumbers and bricklayers. Almost all of them had been trained to expert levels under the direction of Roy's father and now by Roy who was following him. At that time, all trainee crafts required an apprenticeship. This involved the firm signing on a suitably committed and eager young man at only perhaps thirteen or fourteen years of age for a training programme that could take four, five or six years. At the end of this time, a successful trainee came out fully City &

Guilds qualified as a master joiner, electrician or plumber, highly valued not only by the firm but, in those days, by society in general, with the prospect of a decent wage and a career for life for themselves and their families. The apprentices were viewed by Roy, at least, like his own sons, as long as they behaved themselves, which included being invited to his and Gwen's home for celebratory lunches on public feast days. But there was no easy sentimentality or servitude involved. The apprenticeships were hard won and the qualifications that resulted hard earned. The end result benefitted the apprentice as much as the firm, and probably more so in the long term.

The carpenters' "shop" was a wooden workshop built up on stilts above the yard and stuck to the side of the office building like a limpet. There were about fifty wooden steps to climb to access it. The senior carpenter, Mr Hector Munn, was a gnarled master craftsman in his fifties, who had been with the firm for getting on for forty years. The deputy carpenter, Frank Wright, was ten years younger, equally expert but also the star, if that is the right word. The trained apprentice craftsmen they turned out were not simple carpenters – hewers of roofing, fencing and buttresses – but proper joiners: experts in the art of woodcraft, producing in-house staircases, windows and doors. All of these were fashioned with dry mortise and tenon joints, planed to smooth perfection, using wood like a potter might use clay and producing smoothly satisfying house furniture that you could stroke your hand over with a feeling of admiration and no chance of a splinter. The company prided itself in being the epitome of a modern building enterprise.

Henry Dalloway, the leading foreman, was responsible for directing the day-to-day programme of work from the main yard. When he did leave the premises, he could be seen proudly driving the firm's van around town to pick up paints, wallpaper and all decorating materials from Brewer & Sons, or collecting plumbing, screws, nails and all other hardware supplies from the builders' merchant Louis G. Ford in Town Hall Square. This was a reliable builders' merchant chain with outlets found all over the south east, and Strange & Sons were one of their best and most trustworthy customers.

*

On the first of September 1939, just over six months after Roy's father's death, Hitler invaded Poland. World War Two was declared. Both Gwen and Roy did not know how this would affect them personally. Many couples were making the decision to marry hurriedly before the war separated them again, sometimes after only the very briefest of a courtship. Gwen and Roy talked about the situation at length. They were both still without doubt that they wanted to get married and spend the rest of their lives with each other. But Gwen also knew she had a responsibility to her work as a district nurse in Streatham and Roy had only recently been put in the position of being in charge of the family building firm after the death of his father. (He also felt that he should volunteer for the call up to the armed forces, but didn't tell Gwen this at the time.)

They decided to postpone a date for their marriage until it was clear to them both what other responsibilities they were going to be called upon to take on because of this war. With the rest of the British nation, they had much anxiety about how long this war would last for and what might be its outcome. But neither of them had any reservations about the fact that the postponement of their wedding would be only temporary and have no bearing in affecting their love for each other.

CHAPTER 13

Roy did volunteer to sign up to the armed forces soon after World War Two was declared in 1939, although he didn't tell Gwen at the time he had done so. He wasn't confident he would be accepted. He had been a rather frail boy, stunted in health if not in height, by a number of serious infections, including a bout of severe diphtheria when very young, from which his parents had told him later he had nearly died. From then on, he had been somewhat smothered in attention not only by his mother but also by his three older sisters, Marguerite, Muriel and Megan. Throughout his life, he had been concerned that all this attention might have turned him into something of a sissy, having been the only boy in a house full of women. He waited for the decision of the army board with some trepidation; he did not want to be turned down because he was deemed too weak to serve in the armed forces.

When the call came, it did not do so as an appointment to report to the call-up board. Instead, he received a letter telling him that he was working in an essential homeland industry and that his building firm was to be commissioned immediately by the Board of Works for vital coastal defence constructions. These would be a continuation of some of the earlier work his father and the firm had already undertaken in the 1930s, but now the work that was required would be on a much larger scale. He was told the firm was expected to cease its residential building work with immediate effect and concentrate solely on wartime sea defences. Roy was secretly relieved to have received this decision; it would save him the indignity of being rejected by the call-up board for being physically too frail, and instead had put him in a position of being able to work at home in a productive sense towards the war effort. Many of the younger men working for the firm – carpenters, plumbers, electricians, lorry drivers and labourers – had already been called up to the forces. The men that were left were mostly older than Roy, who was now their "guv'nor", but like all the company's employees were still very hardworking, highly experienced and loyal employees. He knew they would be enthused to be taken over by the Board of Trade to undertake vital war work.

The very next morning he received a visit in his office from a Board of Works surveyor. The man arrived in full military dress and introduced himself as Lieutenant Matthew Hunt. He invited Roy to jump into his car, and along with Henry Dalloway, the senior site foreman, the three of them headed straight to the coast. The surveyor drove Roy and his foreman miles along the coastline, taking in Norman's Bay and Pevensey

Bay, stopping at critical spots to mark out areas that the surveyor was interested in. What they were being asked to do, he explained, was to build long lines of anti-tank defences, essentially huge steel wire-reinforced concrete pyramids, which needed to be at close proximity to each other along miles and miles of the shallow beaches that were vulnerable to invasion.

The previous small amount of work the firm had done on some early sea defence projects on the Bexhill beaches had been well received and now they were being asked to step up to a much more ambitious project, which they were expected to undertake full-time. Lieutenant Hunt showed Roy an architect's plan for the details and dimensions of the pyramids. Pouring over the plan that had been laid out in front of him on a large rock, Roy could not help being excited about what was being asked of himself and his men, but secretly was also a little alarmed after having heard the reason for the work. The prospect of an enemy invasion was real and, to hear the surveyor speak, was alarmingly imminent.

'By the way,' the Board of Works surveyor said to Roy before he left, 'please call me Matthew. I always think things work better when relations are friendly; they can still be professional. And it's not as if you are in the army, although the work you and your men are doing is just as important as any soldier's and just as vital in fighting this bloody war. And I'm only a pretend soldier myself in spite of the moniker and the fancy dress!' Then he added, 'I take it it's all right with you that I call you Roy?'

'Of course, Matthew,' Roy replied, happy that he had hit on

such a pleasant chap to work with. When the man arrived unannounced at the office, he had been concerned that the Board of Works surveyor might want to take charge of the work and start bossing him and his men about as soon as he had arrived, but he relaxed, knowing he needn't have worried.

'I have also worked on the basis that "friendly but professional" works best with all my men as well,' Roy said. 'But they still insist on calling me "guv'nor", as they did my father before me, although I'm still in my twenties!'

The two men broke out laughing at this and shook hands to cement their working relationship.

'Needless to say, I'll always be available if you want to discuss any problems you have as they arise, Roy. You only need to shout down the blower, and I'll come down to help. But I'm sure you'll cope fine, old chap. The previous work your team did was first class.'

With that, the lieutenant slapped him on the shoulder and jumped into his army jeep to head further down the coast to his next project.

From that day on, whenever Lieutenant Hunt motored down from the War Department in Whitehall to see him, he always discussed all new projects with Roy first and wanted to know that Roy was happy with the details before they went ahead. After that, he essentially left Roy and his men to carry out the work without his interference.

As soon as they got back to the yard, Roy called all his remaining men together. He told them they had to drop all the domestic work they were doing – building and renovating local houses, painting and decorating, and the like – and to start immediately on the war effort.

'We've been called upon to defend the nation!' Roy concluded in an uncharacteristically melodramatic turn of phrase. 'But I must insist that we are all required to treat this project as top secret. We must be determined to keep what we are doing from enemy spies, which means that we must not even discuss the details of our new war work with our wives and families.'

When he had finished his little speech to the men, a cheer went up and they all threw their caps into the air. At that moment, Roy was immensely proud of his men, who felt the same pride as he did about having been instructed to work on the nation's defences.

When he got home that evening, he telephoned Gwen to tell her that Strange & Sons had now been taken over by the Board of Works. He only spoke in general terms to her about the new plans for coastal defences. He did not want to go into the details he had learnt from the visiting official about the need for anti-tank sea defences and the high likelihood of imminent invasion. In addition to the fact that this work was top secret, he did not feel that it was appropriate to cause her unnecessary alarm about the threat of invasion. He knew that she was already worrying about him, working on the south coast with her a distance away in South London. Roy was practical enough to know that there was nothing he could do himself to stop the invasion happening if it was coming, except of course do his damnedest to ensure that invading forces would not have an easy time coming ashore, and to fight to protect his future wife if they did.

The men set to work with a will almost immediately. Lorries began arriving at the main yard on Terminus Road with cement, sand and gravel, as well as other supplies that they would need to complete the work in double quick time. Henry Dalloway particularly was extremely busy having to find extra space to store all the additional materials. They soon ran out of space at the main yard on Terminus Road, but Henry managed to find an extra piece of land next to their overflow yard to the north of the town on Springfield Road, which he had fenced off securely to store further incoming material. He drove Roy up in his van to inspect the additional yard space he had managed to create. Roy was proud of the speed and enthusiasm the men were showing for the new challenge ahead.

CHAPTER 14

Roy had been receiving increasingly frenetic instructions from the Home Defence Executive, which had been formed under General Sir Edmund Ironside, Commander-in-Chief Home Forces, to organise the defence of Britain in May 1940. The first defence arrangements Ironside had designed had been largely static and focussed on the coastline – "the coastal crust" as it was called – as well as a plan to develop a classical example of "defence in depth", in a series of anti-tank "stop" lines inland that were to be constructed around the capital, London. Although Roy did not get to learn this until after the war – all information of this nature only being meted out to workers at the front line in a piecemeal "need to know" basis – the anti-tank defences he and his men were constructing were part of the longest and most heavily fortified coastal defence line ever planned. It was named the General Headquarters anti-tank line – the GHQ Line. The portion of the coastal defences they were building was only a small element of a major plan projected to run along this part of southern England and then right up around London and northwards up the east coast as far as Yorkshire.

One afternoon in the middle of July, Roy was walking along the beach with Henry Dalloway inspecting the work that had been undertaken that morning. He had become concerned about the quality of both the cement for the concrete blocks they were constructing and the steel wire they were having to use to reinforce these. He and Henry had cut open a number of the sacks of cement that had been delivered from central supplies that morning to look at their contents. Running handfuls of the stuff through their fingers, they were disturbed to find that there seemed to be as much dust in the sacks as pure cement.

Henry had also shown Roy the lorry load consignment of steel wires that had been dropped on the beach the evening before. Most of this seemed to have been obtained from second-hand scrap metal that had been recycled from the fencing and gateways of London houses and parks. They knew that there was a national shortage of steel and that scrap metal was being collected from wherever it could be found for projects like theirs, but a lot of this steel wiring consignment appeared to be badly rusted already.

In the end, there was nothing they could do about the poor-quality materials they were being supplied with. As they walked along the beach, Henry pointed out to Roy that the concrete blocks constructed during the previous few days all seemed to have set well. They could only hope that the anti-tank defences would fulfil the function for which they were intended, should the need arise, even though they also hoped that they would never be required. As they looked up from their inspection work, Roy saw a convoy of military vehicles and staff cars drawing up unannounced on the beach road above them.

'*Bloody hell*,' Roy heard Henry Dalloway whispering in his ear. '*It's Winnie!*'

The door of the leading staff car was thrown open by an adjutant and the Prime Minister stepped out, wearing his black bowler hat, cigar in hand, accompanied by an army general who Roy was later to learn was General Brooke. The visiting party strode down onto the beach, Churchill nodding as he passed Roy and Henry, who were, by now, standing stiffly to attention, their arms rigid by their sides with their thumbs to the front of their clutched fists, as if they were part of the British Army themselves. Churchill swept onto the beach with his retinue in his wake, and General Brooke started to point out the work that had already been completed east and west along this part of the coast of Pevensey Bay. After they had passed, Roy looked round to see that the group of twenty or so of his men on this part of the beach had also lined up spontaneously, as if they too were part of a guard of honour on the parade ground.

The adjutant brought a wooden lectern out from the back of one of the following vehicles and placed it on the shingle. A large plan of works was secured onto it by bull clips, its borders fluttering in the sea breeze over the sides of the lectern. The two men walked back up the beach and stood behind the lectern, pouring over the plan in deep discussion. General Brooke was evidently indicating the details of the further essential works he considered to be required. Churchill stood next to him, grunting occasionally in agreement, and taking a draw on his cigar from time to time, before exhaling the smoke into the Sussex sea air.

When they had finished, Churchill, with his hands clasped behind his back, walked back with Brooke towards the staff car. Roy hoped the Prime Minister had been satisfied with the work they had been reviewing. Before he climbed back into his car, Churchill stopped, with one foot on the running board, and turned back towards Roy and the rest of the gang.

'Keep up the good work, men. Your country needs you!' he exhorted them, before he settled himself back into the rear of the staff car and tucked a tartan blanket around his legs. As the car drew off, the men roared in unison, throwing their caps into the air to show their respect to their nation's wartime leader. Churchill heard their reaction to his visit and turned and gave a wry grin through the open car window to his audience, raising his right hand in the by then familiar open "V" sign as the car turned inland and disappeared out of sight.

Two days later, on the nineteenth of July 1940, Roy read in a small paragraph in the daily newspaper that, after spending that afternoon with General Brooke on the south coast, Churchill had stood down General Ironside as Head of the Home Defence Executive. The paper did not go into any detail or explain why this change had been made, for obvious reasons, but the next day, the Ministry of Works surveyor Lieutenant Hunt paid Roy a visit to explain what had taken place.

Apparently Churchill had not been satisfied with the progress being made in the construction of defences under Ironside and had replaced him with Brooke. Brooke was convinced that more concentration should be placed on defending the country with the "coastal crust", part of which Roy and his team were constructing. He had also proposed that anti-tank islands should be established along the already constructed inland stop lines, and the Prime Minister had agreed with Brooke the next steps that should be taken to defend the nation from invasion.

'Nothing to do with your work, old chap,' Matthew Hunt said the next day, as he noticed Roy looking a little downcast. 'Don't take it personally. What you and your men have achieved is admirable, and I have told the Ministry of Works so. What took place yesterday was just a bit of wartime politics above the heads of us foot soldiers!' he laughed, slapping Roy on the shoulder in his usual manner as he left to get back into his car.

Whatever the politics of the matter, it was clear to Roy that even more work was coming their way and that the speed of building the coastline defences would need to be accelerated significantly. He knew they had to cope. It would play a vital role in the defence of the nation.

CHAPTER 15

One day in early October 1940, Roy drove out to Pevensey Bay with Matthew Hunt to inspect the recent work they had just completed and to plan the next phase of construction with the Board of Works surveyor. As always, Hunt was happy with the work. He thanked Roy and his men for the work they had done that year. Their sea defences now stretched over a considerable length of that part of the coast. Looking west towards Eastbourne, Roy could see the bay stretching away for hundreds of yards and knew that there was still a huge amount of work ahead of them. But it was good for him and his men to have someone who understood how hard they had been working and showed them his appreciation of the fact.

After Hunt had left to go back to London, Roy sat in the small mizzen hut the men had erected for themselves to take their breaks in out of the blazing sun, driving rain and high winds, all of which had been thrown at them that year. He unwrapped the greaseproof paper package containing the sandwiches that he had made for himself that morning and unscrewed the Thermos flask of coffee, sharing a cup with Henry Dalloway, who was sitting having his lunch with him. The two men were pleased with the work that had been completed so far, but talked about the challenge of the considerable amount of coastline that still had to be tackled.

As they sat eating lunch, they paid hardly any attention to the air battle that was being fought in the skies above them. The so-called Battle of Britain had been raging in the skies above for three months now. He and his men had become used to the dog fights going on between the RAF Spitfires and Hurricanes and the German Luftwaffe in the skies overhead, so much so that they barely looked up to watch what was going on, determined not to let the fighting above them interrupt the progress they were making in the construction of the coastal defences.

The day before, however, they had seen a Spitfire, hit from the rear, start plummeting towards the sea in front of them, flames licking out of its cockpit and black smoke issuing from its fuselage. They had watched in horror for the few seconds it took, as the pilot attempted to bail out, but too late, before the plane crashed into the waves. His body was brought ashore later that afternoon by the RAF marine rescue. The men had worked on, but their manner was subdued as they did so. If they had cared to forget for a time what the purpose of their work was, they had been reminded now.

The next day after lunch, Roy said goodbye to Henry and the other men on his work contingent and got back into his car. He had to get back to the office in Bexhill to make a number of urgent calls to the Board of Works department. He had become relieved to find that, with the war in Europe grinding on, the amount of paper work and bureaucracy had been pared down to the minimum – essentially, the board had come to trust him to get on with the work that had been commissioned. But there were always small issues that had to be ironed out as things progressed.

Roy drove home eastwards, turning right off Sea Road onto Pevensey Marsh Road, the wide three-lane concrete road that traversed the Pevensey Marshes that lay either side of the road towards Bexhill. His was the only car on the road that afternoon and he put his foot down on the accelerator to increase his speed to a fair lick. As he looked ahead, he suddenly realised that there was a fighter plane closing in on him from the opposite direction. He saw with alarm that it was descending nearer and nearer to the road and was coming straight at him. He could see at once that it was not one of the RAF planes that regularly patrolled the coastline, but a German Messerschmitt Bf 109, which he recognised from its closed canopy. He had nowhere to turn off onto from the long straight road and nothing he could do to take evasive action. As the plane approached at speed, it opened its machine guns and strafed him from only a couple of hundred feet off the ground. He could even see the face of the pilot looking down at him from the cockpit. Roy ducked his head onto the steering wheel and placed one arm across his eyes, actions which he realised afterwards would have been no help in saving him if the car had received a direct hit. The plane roared over him and banked away back out to sea.

He pulled onto the verge, slammed on the brakes and jumped out to inspect the car. Miraculously, the car had not copped a single bullet. The tyres were all inflated and, on rapid inspection, he could see hardly a single mark on the bodywork. He jumped back into the car, hurriedly engaging the clutch and pulling off into the first small lane he came across, expecting the plane to come back to have another go at him. But luckily there was no sign of it returning, and he drove slowly back home on a circuitous route on minor roads across the marshes, shaken but elated that he had survived this small part of "his" war.

He didn't tell Gwen what had happened to him that afternoon, when he spoke to her on the phone that evening. He knew she was anxious enough about his safety all the time he was out at work along the beaches. There was no point in worrying her unduly now.

CHAPTER 16

Gwen and Roy finally married on the third of September 1942. Gwen was thirty-one years old by this time. Before the war, she would have been considered unusually old to get married – a "spinster". But in the middle of World War Two, that sort of consideration had been put to one side. Gwen was not alone in having been determined to pursue a professional career before getting married, and for many other women there was of course the fact that lots of the men of marrying age were away from home fighting in the war. The young women left behind them had got on with their lives, in the absence of their men, forging a role for themselves in the civilian war effort. In the push to manufacture weapons and ammunition, to keep the factories and the farms producing to the maximum, and in bringing in the harvest for the latter, the women were all also fighting the enemy in the most determined ways they could find.

They were married by the minister at the Congregational church in Bexhill and afterwards had a small reception in the

Granville Hotel near the sea front. Both Gwen's parents and Roy's mother attended, as did Roy's three sisters and as many of Gwen's brothers and sisters who were living locally and not fighting abroad. Her brothers Ray and Don had joined up for the RAF and were fighting as ground crew somewhere in Europe, although no-one knew where. Her aunt Hettie and her husband also came down on the train from Streatham for the wedding, and Gwen was delighted that they had been able to attend. Her father had eventually got over his resistance to the fact that she had chosen to become a nurse, against his strongly stated wishes, and admitted to her at the wedding reception that he was proud of what she had achieved. This made her blush with pride as he kissed her rather awkwardly. She was so happy that she had redeemed herself in his eyes.

A number of Roy's team from his building firm Strange & Sons, including Henry Dalloway, his senior foreman, and Basil Chart, his office assistant, had been invited to the wedding and the reception. They stood around the sides of the dining hall at the hotel reception looking a little embarrassed as they clutched their beer glasses. Gwen couldn't help giggling as she pointed this out to Roy. As he laughed with his new wife, Roy thought to himself that it was funny how, since his enforced takeover as manager of the company by the unexpected death of his father, and in spite of his previous reservations, he had now grown into the role and was enjoying it immensely. He had come to realise that this occupation suited him well, after all, and had abandoned any further thought of forging a different career in the electronics industry.

Roy had asked the youngest of Gwen's brothers, Stuart Oddy – who happened to be back on a short home leave – to be his best man. Stuart looked very smart in his RAF dress uniform, with shining black belt and boots. Both he and Roy gave charming and witty speeches at the reception. Gwen looked radiant in the wedding dress her aunt Hettie had made for her, and Roy looked as handsome and debonair as she had ever seen him, with his black hair sleeked down and neatly parted on one side and his morning suit fitting his thin frame perfectly.

They went to their new home, the semi-detached house on Glenthorn Road, directly after their wedding. They had decided that it was not the time to go travelling on any sort of honeymoon and that setting up their new home would be a perfect way of starting their married life. Roy carried her across the threshold for her first visit – he had not allowed her to go and see it while it was being refurbished – and Gwen was delighted with their new abode. Roy and his men had renovated and decorated it beautifully and had even laboured hard to make the garden look splendid. It was a modest two-bedroom semi-detached house, which nevertheless had cost Roy £800 to buy, although he had not mentioned to Gwen how much he had paid for it. That was all of his savings and more, the balance of which he had borrowed from the bank. He knew it would take him some years to pay off the debt.

*

They had not been living in their new home on Glenthorn Road for very long after their wedding when they received notice from the government that they were to be evacuated from there to somewhere safer than the town of Bexhill-on-Sea.

Very soon after receiving this news, Roy and Gwen were moved to a tiny cottage in Hooe, a small village just inland from the Pevensey Marshes. When they had received the letter informing them they were to be evacuated from their home in Bexhill, they had no idea what this had meant. They had been wondering whether, like many others they knew, they may be moved anywhere in Great Britain, from Land's End to John O'Groats. As it turned out, Hooe was only a few miles west of the town and from their house on Glenthorn Road. It appeared that the work Roy was engaged in was important enough for the Board of Works to want to protect him from even the remote chance of threat from air attacks. Gwen was not keen for them to have to undergo this change in their lives, especially since they had only just got the house on Glenthorn Road set up to their satisfaction. But once she saw the place they were going to, she became quite excited about the move and set about with enthusiasm to make the charming little thatched cottage that had been allocated to them their new, if temporary, home.

CHAPTER 17

Living in the tiny thatched cottage in the small village of Hooe was perhaps the happiest time Gwen and Roy were to spend together in all their married life. The village was situated right on the corner of the Pevensey Marshes, near the bottom of the hill leading up to Wartling village. The quaint old cottage they found themselves in by chance was charming, and the village a sleepy rural retreat. They never did quite understand how it came to be that they had been evacuated from their town house in Bexhill-on-Sea to such an idyllic situation only a few miles west of the town.

When they first arrived to look over the place, Roy told Gwen that they had probably been offered the cottage because it was situated very near to his essential war defences work along the coast. And it was true, he could walk out of the village and arrive on the beach, which was less than a mile away, in about twenty minutes. But he still needed the car to reach the farther reaches of Norman's Bay to the west of Hooe, not to mention to travel to Pevensey Bay further along from there. But after they had seen the place, they did not question why they had been billeted there any more.

They could not believe their luck. It had been a mild spring and a dry summer in 1943 and that July was idyllic. Roy and Gwen could walk out onto the marshes and explore together in the warm weather, taking a blanket and a picnic with them on sunny evenings and weekends. They felt they had landed in a *Shangri-La*, their imaginary paradise on earth, far away from the war that continued to rage in the rest of Europe and the Far East. When Roy was away all day working on building the defences, Gwen would take a basket and wander out on her own, picking cowslips and filling tubs with blackberries in August. She became at home exploring the Pevensey Marshes, which she found fascinating. Roy was delighted that Gwen's anxiety about his safety and the war in general had lifted from her, and he would come back from the beaches in the evening to find his wife happy and excited, no longer anxious and depressed as she had been in recent times.

Some days, Gwen would walk for hours across the large area of wetland grazing meadows, jumping over the network of ditches when she came to them. She would stoop down and cup both hands together at each ditch she came to, scooping up a handful of water to inspect what she had found. She got to recognise the freshwater molluscs, her favourite being the shining ram's-horn snail. She knew these were rare species and would always return them lovingly to their ditch once she'd had the chance to inspect them. Some days she would walk miles to the north of the Pevensey Levels towards the villages of Boreham Street or Herstmonceux. She would take a break, hiding behind a convenient bush and wait patiently for a lapwing to land nearby, with its rich colours and regal head feathers. She asked Roy to bring her a book about the area from the Bexhill library when he next went into town. When he brought this back for her, she would sit up late into the evening reading about the flora and fauna that the marshes contained.

Some evenings, she and Roy would walk down to the Lamb Inn on Top Road and have a pint of beer in the rustic sixteenth-century pub. They were new arrivals, but the locals never ceased to make them feel welcome and told them they hoped they would stay. Roy was delighted to come home from a long day's work and find Gwen happy and impatient to tell him about where she had been and what she had found while he was away at work.

The happiness of their time living together there was topped when one evening at the end of October 1943, she told him she was pregnant with their first child. Soon after that, they decided to move back to their town house in Bexhill. They were both sad to leave their idyllic village of Hooe behind but realised that it would be better not to be too far away from the town when the time came for Gwen to give birth.

CHAPTER 18

Gwen and Roy were immensely excited about the forthcoming birth of their first child, and Roy arranged with Dr Winchester, their family doctor, that Gwen should be admitted to a nursing home north of the Old Town in Bexhill to give birth when the time came. They went to visit there at the beginning of June, when Gwen was already eight months pregnant, and were very happy with the place and especially the midwife who had been assigned to look after Gwen at her time of need. With all her nursing experience, Gwen could recognise a caring nurse when she met one and immediately took to midwife Alice as a professional she could trust. Alice arranged to come and see Gwen at home, now that her expected date of delivery was getting close, and the two of them hit it off at once. Gwen told Roy that she had made a new friend, one she would like to keep contact with after her child was born. He was relieved that Gwen was happy and optimistic about the approaching birth and that made him happy and reassured that all would be well.

Their son Michael was born on the sixth of July 1944. Gwen had had a prolonged labour, but Alice had reassured Roy during it that this was quite normal for a first birth. The labour had been more painful than Gwen could have ever imagined it would be, but the baby was born fully formed and alive and kicking, with Alice's supportive professional help. The anxieties and apprehension that went with any childbirth, especially their first, soon dissolved and Roy was able to leave his wife and child in good hands when he went back home to get some sleep himself later that night.

When he telephoned very early that next morning, Roy was delighted to hear from Alice that all was well and Gwen was breastfeeding Michael as they spoke.

'Please give my wife all my love, sister,' he said. 'Tell her I'll be up to visit her – and Michael, of course! – this evening when I've finished work.'

With that, he replaced the receiver and went off to shave, a happy man. He left the house early to head for the beaches.

Early on in the war, in addition to his full-time work supervising the building of anti-tank defences along their part of the Sussex coast, Roy had also signed up as an Air Raid Precautions (ARP) warden. The ARP wardens were responsible for protecting the civilian population from the danger of air raids. Roy was tasked with enforcing the blackout in his section of the town after dark. All householders had been required to install heavy curtains and shutters to prevent light escaping and therefore making them a marker for enemy bombers to locate their targets. In practice, this small Sussex coastal town was not a strategic target for the bombers, who were invariably intent on bombing the capital, London, and the factories and ports of other major cities.

Most of the damage that Bexhill had suffered had come from aircraft off-loading any remaining bombs they had on board as they returned home from bombing raids on London and other cities. This meant that any bombs that fell on Bexhill were likely to be incidental but in spite of this, were no less lethal for their indeterminate targets. Nevertheless, it was his duty to report on bombing incidents, ensure people were directed to shelters, check gas masks and evacuate areas around unexploded bombs. He would liaise with the police, ambulance drivers, and fire brigade and rescue parties when necessary. On one or two occasions, he had personally rescued people from bombed-out premises before any of the other services had arrived on the scene.

One night a few days after Michael's birth, Roy arrived home after dark and, having hastily consumed his supper and a cup of cocoa, he pulled on his dark blue overalls and the red on black ARP badge on his upper arm. He thrust his helmet on his head and adjusted the chin strap as he left the house for that night's duty. He was planning to complete the first couple of hours of blackout duty before making his way up to the Old Town and the nursing home to pay a quick visit to his wife Gwen and their new born son on his break.

At about ten p.m., Roy had completed his blackout

surveillance and was making his way up through the Old Town towards the nursing home at the top of Hastings Road. As he did so, he was aware of the roar of an enemy bomber passing overhead, on its way back towards the English Channel. The roar of the plane was followed a few seconds later by an almighty explosion somewhere right in front of him. He fell headfirst onto the grass verge, partly because of the shockwave of the bomb but also because of the avoidance protection training that came into his actions these days as a reflex. After the immediate impact, he raised himself from the ground and dusted himself down, uninjured. Looking up, he could see smoke arising from the direction he was heading.

Breaking into a run, Roy set off at a pace and reached the bottom of Hastings Road, where the nursing home housing his wife and new son was situated. Running now at a sprint, he reached the place and stood in dismay in front of it.

The nursing home was badly damaged, with the wing on the left completely demolished and flames and smoke still engulfing the central section of the building. As he stood looking at the scene in disbelief, the Bexhill fire engine – "Lady Kitty" as it was known locally, for what ridiculous reason he could not explain at this moment – arrived, followed immediately by two ambulances, their bells jangling frenetically. Roy ran towards the right-hand wing of the damaged building where he knew Gwen and baby Michael were. As he rushed up the stairs, one of the nurses was coming down, leading Gwen to safety with the baby in her arms. He ran to them and embraced them both in utter relief. Mother and baby were covered from head to foot in dust and plaster but were apparently unharmed. He led them gently to safety out of the building.

As Roy stood comforting his wife and baby child in the front garden, he looked up and saw stretcher parties bringing bodies out of the wreckage of the nursing home in front of them. The first stretcher to emerge carried the body of a young mother, still clutching tightly to her newborn baby. Both had died locked together in this embrace. He shielded the scene from Gwen by turning towards her and wrapping his coat around her. As he looked back, the next stretcher to emerge carried the body of another woman. He could see she was dressed in a torn and blood-streaked nurse's uniform. He left his wife and went quietly towards the stretcher party, to ask if he could be of assistance. As he got there, he could see that the dead woman's head was not covered. He recognised her at once. It was midwife Alice.

At that moment Roy knew he wanted to get Gwen and their newborn baby away from this scene of horrible, pointless carnage. He had become used to helping out at such incidents on bomb sites in town for a while now, but, horrific as they were, these had always involved other peoples' tragedies. This one had suddenly become personal. He beckoned to one of the ambulance drivers who had just arrived. The man recognised Roy and his ARP armband. He helped him gently guide Gwen with her baby Michael into the ambulance and, having satisfied himself that they were all shocked but physically unharmed, drove them slowly away from the scene of destruction and back to their own home.

Over the next few days, Roy did not go back to work on the beach. He sent a message to Henry Dalloway explaining what had happened and asking him to carry on with the work without him. He knew he could trust the man to do so. The following hours and days he spent with Gwen and their baby Michael were times of joy, mixed with times of guilt and deep depression. Gwen could not understand why she and her baby had survived the brutal air raid attack. She felt guilty that she had been spared at the expense of the other mothers and babies who had not survived. In particular, she grieved for the loss of the angel Alice and for her loved ones, even though she had not got to meet them.

For some time, Roy was concerned that this tragic incident might be the thing that would lead to a prolonged period of postnatal depression for Gwen. He had heard about this awful condition. The wife of one of his men had suffered from it very badly, to the point where she'd had to be removed from her baby and sent to a special hospital for some months. He had worried even before the shock of that evening in the nursing home that Gwen's personality might make her prone to this. He had known her long enough by now to know that she was prone to periods of unexplained depression, alternating with times when she could be extraordinarily happy, even a little unnaturally euphorically so on some occasions. But he was relieved to find that, depressed by the events in the nursing home bombing as she was, there was no sign whatsoever of Gwen rejecting baby Michael in any way. Indeed, since she realised that her baby could have been killed by the bomb, he had become even more precious to her, if that was possible. She was breastfeeding him without difficulty and Roy was relieved to see that she was having no problem bonding with their child. She would sing to him constantly while feeding him, even though the songs she sang were often rather sad ones.

So eventually, after days of mourning, Gwen's guilt and depression finally lifted. Joy in her newborn child won then, in spite of the war.

CHAPTER 19

The war was finally over, although the country was still having to cope with the social and economic hardship it had caused. The year after the war ended, Gwen gave birth to their daughter Elizabeth Mary, who was born in October 1946. In 1948, with two young children, Gwen found herself pregnant again. She and Roy decided that they would need more space for their growing family and found a larger house on Cranston Avenue, in the west part of town. They were sorry to leave what had been their very first home together on Glenthorn Road, but they were running out of space and needed more. Apart from anything else, they had a bigger garden at the back of the new house, which gave some space for the children to play safely. It was there that their second son Geoffrey John was born in March 1949.

Following the end of the war, life remained difficult for the whole nation, with ration books still around into the early 1950s. During this time, Roy and Gwen used part of their larger garden to keep hens, and the children all enjoyed the deep orange-yolked eggs that they produced. They would regularly sit down to tea to consume the boiled eggs and bread and butter soldiers that their mother had prepared for them to dip into these home-produced, delicious eggs. In the post-war years, they were seen as a real treat.

Although very young at the time, Geoffrey could vividly remember waking up very early one summer morning (it was probably only about four a.m.) to the sight of his father in his striped pyjamas leaning out of the back landing window shaking his fist and shouting at a fox that had buried its way into the hen house, wreaking carnage, which had been announced by the chickens squawking loudly and at a high pitch as they fought for their lives, to no avail. The hens were a precious possession, and the loss of even a part of the collection a great blow to the family.

CHAPTER 20

At the end of 1953, with business picking up for Roy and another child on the way, the family moved to their last home, "West Winds", situated at number forty-four Terminus Avenue, Bexhill-on-Sea. This was a fairly substantial but not pretentious five-bedroom detached house also on the west side of town. It was on the residential road that led away from Terminus Road, where the offices and yard of Strange & Sons were situated. The other end of Terminus Avenue terminated at Collington Woods, a small but, for the children, rather exciting wooded area that provided them with many hours of exploration, games and enjoyment. The house was not exactly the sort of place that millionaire Larkin – whose building firm was Roy's chief competitor in the town – would have aspired to. But it was a comfortable family home that Roy and Gwen had been able to achieve for the family as a result of their hard work.

The house had a grass-covered front lawn with a modest concrete drive on one side leading up to the garage. In the back, there was a vegetable garden and a small area of fruit trees. Gwen worked hard to improve the garden and Roy could see that she found the work therapeutic. There was always more that needed doing, however. When they were older, the children would agree to help their mother or father by pushing the mower around and doing other basics jobs in the garden, but probably with less than the good grace their parents deserved to have shown to them in these reasonable tasks.

One of the family's earliest childhood excitements was the arrival of their first black and white television. This took place on Saturday, the fifth of March 1954; it happened to be Geoffrey's fifth birthday. He was laid up in bed wheezing with some sort of chest infection when he heard clattering and banging outside and, looking towards his bedroom window, saw two men climbing up outside on ladders to fix the "H" television mast to the chimney stack on the roof above. The excitement of this was indescribable, bettered only later that afternoon by his parents allowing him downstairs at about four o'clock to watch the Saturday sports on the television. *Sportsview* was the afternoon sports programme presented by Peter Dimmock, featuring all the latest news and teleprinter results of that afternoon's football matches.

Looking back, the impact and novelty of all this was immense. The fact that they were the first family on the road to have a television, and probably one of the first in the whole town, did not come into it. It was at that time just so new and different and unspeakably modern. The children had no idea at the time that their father Roy had been involved in developing the early television receivers produced by Pye some twenty years before.

Gwen had been allocated a district midwife to supervise her last pregnancy. The woman, Janet, visited her at home throughout the pregnancy and was pleasant enough on the surface. But Gwen found her a little brusque and did not take to her much. For one thing, the woman was always in a hurry. She would bustle into the house, roll up her sleeves and snap on elasticated cuffs to the end of them, before she started to examine Gwen's abdomen. She didn't wait around long after she had finished her examination, and there was never any time for a cup of tea or a pleasant chat. Gwen found this all a little discouraging. The contrast in attitude between this midwife and the care she had received when looked after by the midwives when Michael, Elizabeth and Geoffrey had been born was marked. She still grieved for the loss of her first midwife, the angel Alice.

Gwen was forty-three by the time Paul was born in 1954 and she was labelled an "elderly multigravida" by midwife Janet who attended her. Gwen knew from her professional training that this was the technically correct term for her obstetric history – becoming pregnant after the age of forty was known to be at increased risk, both to the mother and the newborn child. It was not a term she would use herself in front of a pregnant lady though, she thought at the time. She gave birth to Paul at home, in the middle of the night some days past her due date. The birth was without complications, nevertheless.

Geoffrey, who was five and a half by then, remembered

waking up in the early hours of the first of September 1954 to a mewing sound, coming in some distress and increasing intensity from the room next door. It was immediately obvious to him that the noise he was hearing was the result of his sister's cat, Paddy Paws, being caught in some emergency or distressful situation. He sat up in bed and hollered to his father to alert him of this. On hearing his cries, Roy came running in with excited tears in his eyes to explain that what Geoffrey was actually hearing were the first earthly notes of his younger brother Paul, who had just emerged at full term from his mother's womb.

CHAPTER 21

As time went by, Roy could see that, with the house and four young children to look after, Gwen needed some time to herself for parts of the week. Rather than hiring a professional nanny, he hit on the idea of asking one of Gwen's unmarried older sisters, Freda, if she would take on the role part-time. Freda was a pleasant lady whom life seemed to have passed by a little. She had never had a "young man", let alone a husband, and was by now in her late forties. She was a simple but caring person, and Roy had a hunch that she would be an ideal family member to help with the care of the house and their four children.

Freda had recently moved in with her even older sister Elsie in a bungalow ideal for two single ladies on Gunter's Lane, on the north side of the town. Elsie worked as a secretary for Gwen's younger brother Stuart Oddy in his flour mill business in Robertsbridge and was unlikely to have the time to take up additional part-time work. In any case, Roy found Elsie a little sour or even grumpy at times and wasn't sure how she would take to looking after the children, or indeed them to her.

Freda agreed to come and help immediately, and Roy saw at once that he'd been right in thinking she would fit the bill. She took up the work enthusiastically, insisting that she didn't want to be paid to help them. But Roy was insistent that he should give her the going rate for her work, and Freda finally agreed, which pleased himself and Gwen. They both knew that she had very little money to live on. Before long, Freda was part of their extended family, cleaning, shopping and cooking as well as looking after the children, to the point where Gwen had to stipulate that Freda should have time of her own off during the week as well.

'It's a real treat to have Freda help me with the house and children,' Gwen said to Roy, as they were sitting in front of the fire together one evening after Freda had left and the children had gone to bed.

'I'm pleased you feel like that,' Roy replied. 'I knew she'd be a big help. In fact, I think she's getting as much or more out of the arrangement than you are! I can't help noticing that the sparkle has come back into her eyes at last. She's got something to live for rather than the really dreary spinster's rut her life had got into.'

'Don't say that!' Gwen retorted. 'She can't help the fact that she never got married herself.' Gwen was always supportive of all her brothers and sisters, especially Freda. 'But I do agree that her life can't be all that fun at times, living with bossy Elsie.'

Roy burst out laughing. Gwen clearly had the same

impression about her oldest sister as he did, although she had never passed on her opinion of Elsie to him before.

'So, my dear, what do you want to do with your new-found freedom?' he asked her, with rather a tease in his voice.

'Oh, I don't know,' she replied. 'You know me, I'm not one for joining in with coffee mornings and bridge evenings and that sort of thing. There's plenty going on at the church I could give more time to. But I thought it might be interesting to branch out a bit. What do you think about me volunteering to help at the Red Cross centre on London Road?'

'Darling, that's a terrific idea! I'm sure they'd be delighted to have you and would make good use of all your nursing experience.' Roy was rather surprised to hear her suggestion. She had obviously been thinking it through for a while. So the very next day, she gave the local Red Cross centre a ring and, before she knew it, two weeks later was joining in with the local branch ladies, most of whom were new to her. It was getting her out of the house and giving her a separate interest in life, which Roy had hoped would be the case. She veritably threw herself into the role, which not only entailed giving first aid assistance at various events taking place in the town from time to time, but also putting on weekly lunches at the centre for people with mental health and other issues. Gwen was an excellent cook and particularly enjoyed being responsible for the cooking and serving of lunches for at least thirty people every Wednesday lunchtime. Her colleagues recognised her value with warmth and admiration.

One Tuesday, Gwen found herself doing a shift at the Red Cross centre that morning. She was on her own and started looking around to see what she could do to make herself useful. She happened to look into the dressings cupboard. She saw to her horror that things were all over the place, different items all mixed up together, rolls of bandages and packs of dressings on top of each other and on the floor of the cupboard where they had fallen.

'Some of these must be years old,' she said to herself. Those dressings that were brown at the edges and the elasticated bandages that had completely lost their elastic stretch she scooped up and threw into the bin. She busied herself going through the rest of the rather meagre store, arranging the bandages, tourniquets and dressings and so on into more logical, easy to locate groups on the shelves. It wasn't quite the same as preparing her theatre for the next operating session or counting the swabs ready for Mr Tanner's surgery, she laughed to herself, but it was something she knew she still had a flair for.

Madge, the Red Cross centre supervisor, arrived later in the morning. Gwen said hello to her and went out into the kitchen in the back of the shop to wash up the cups and clean the sink from the staff coffee the day before. A few minutes later, Madge came into the kitchen to talk to her.

'I see you've been clearing up the dressings cupboard, Mrs Baines.'

In spite of the fact that Gwen had been working as a volunteer for over six weeks now, Madge persisted in calling her and all the other volunteers by their surnames. The rest of the lady volunteers all used first names with each other. Gwen had sensed from the first that this was an approach that Madge adopted to emphasise the fact she was in charge. She was also prone to highlight the fact that she was a fully trained first aider at every opportunity. On one occasion she had told Gwen and the other ladies how the first aid course had been very difficult – "definitely not a piece of cake" – but that she had passed the test in spite of this.

'I would be grateful if you would pass it by me before rearranging things,' she now instructed Gwen.

Gwen looked at the woman, dumbfounded at her officiousness, but said nothing in reply. She had not told any of the volunteer ladies that she was a trained nurse, let alone that she had been a senior theatre sister and a district nurse. She had not even mentioned these facts to Madge who had interviewed her when she had volunteered as a helper. She hadn't wanted to sound cocky.

'Sorry,' was all she said to the woman now. She turned away to continue the washing up, not wanting to show Madge the tears that were welling up in her eyes. *What is wrong with me?* she asked herself silently. She had never been an arrogant or boastful person, but these days she seemed to have lost any self-esteem she once had. Certainly she'd had that at St James', without being pushy. But she seemed to have lost it all now, for reasons that she could not grasp. Rather than fight the woman, she just felt resigned and pathetic.

When Roy got home that evening, Gwen burst into tears.

'Darling, what is it, my love?' he asked, putting his arms around her as she sobbed into his chest. When she had gathered herself, Gwen sat on the sofa holding his hand and told him about the upset with Madge. It all sounded so petty now as she recounted the facts. She knew it was, but she couldn't rise above it.

Roy said nothing but sat with his brow furrowed with concern. 'I'll put the kettle on,' he said, getting up and kissing her on the forehead as he did so.

CHAPTER 22

Gwen did not acquire a car until the mid-1960s, more than thirty years after she had met and married Roy. But she already had a full driving licence. In the 1930s, a driving licence was awarded to any person who applied on paper in the correct way and was not dependent on the demonstration of any driving proficiency, let alone the passing of a formal driving test. Gwen had applied for a licence in 1935, thinking it might come in handy at some time in her career as a nurse. But, as it happened, she never had the need to drive a car professionally. She still kept the old bike that she had used as a district nurse to take her around Streatham in their garage. She had not ridden this since those days but still cherished it for sentimental reasons. So, thirty years after being issued with a driving licence, which was still legally valid even though she had not ventured behind the wheel of a car with it once, Roy bought her a round black Morris Minor 1000, licence number NAP 310, and, after a brief demonstration by him, off she went in it without any real lessons.

Geoffrey, who was fifteen by then, was the one his mother usually recruited to accompany her on any journey she chose to make. She was at least aware enough to know that she ought to have someone to support her when behind the wheel. These journeys left Geoffrey with nightmare memories. He found himself sitting next to her in the front passenger seat, white knuckled and in fear. As far as he was concerned, his mother had no perception of how to control the vehicle and what he was later to describe to his father Roy as "complete left-to-right dissociation".

'When I suggested, "turn left here, Mum",' he said to his father after the first trip, 'she turned the wheel violently to the right, sometimes into the path of other oncoming vehicles. When I told her to "turn right here", she would veer over towards the left side of the road and nearly mount the pavement.' Roy listened to his middle son, somewhat perturbed.

On one particularly harrowing day, swinging into their own front drive after returning from the shops, Geoff shouted at the top of his voice, "Mind the gate post, Mum!" only to hear the sickening thud and feel the jarring shudder as the front offside wheel arch crunched into contact with the wooden gate post. Afterwards, Gwen admitted to Roy that she had been shaken by that experience. Geoffrey certainly had been. From then on, Gwen used the car very little, until eventually Roy agreed with her that she really didn't need to use it, and it was sold on.

Roy continued to drive everywhere he went. He favoured Morris Oxford cars by then, starting off with a large, round black model and then with time graduating to a rather sleek pale blue Morris Oxford newer version, AAP 313E. Roy took driving very seriously, aware what a dangerous pastime it could be and particularly feeling the need to protect his family when he was driving them anywhere. He became proud of his competence behind the wheel and his safety record when driving. In time, he applied to the Institute of Advanced Motoring to take their rigorous Advanced Driving test and passed it at the first time of taking. He was one of the earliest motorists in the country to do so.

Over the years that followed, the family were to take their annual summer holidays by car, initially to the Lake District and the Scottish Highlands, before branching off to foreign holidays in Germany, Austria and Switzerland. In those days, when not many did so, travelling by car on the "wrong side" of the road on the continent was an exciting adventure. As soon as his eldest son Michael passed his seventeenth birthday, Roy took him onto the roads with his preliminary driving licence and taught him the best driving rules. Michael passed his driving test at the first attempt and very soon was acting as Roy's co-driver for their family holidays across Europe.

CHAPTER 23

In 1962, an international crisis erupted following a confrontation between the United States and the Soviet Union. The United States had deployed missiles in Turkey and Italy, within striking distance of the Soviet Union. The Soviet Union's response was to reach an agreement with the Cuban leader Fidel Castro to place its own ballistic missiles on the island of Cuba, within threatening distance of the USA, to resist any attempt at invasion the Americans might be considering. These events were to trigger the so-called "Cuban missile crisis". The whole world became gripped in fear by the prospect of a possible global nuclear war.

Finally, towards the end of October that year, the news broke on the television that the crisis had finally been resolved and the prospect of worldwide nuclear war leading to the probable annihilation of mankind had been averted, due to an agreement brokered by President John F Kennedy with his Soviet counterpart Nikita Khrushchev. An almost audible cry of relief could be heard across the world.

Roy and his children rushed into the living room to hear the announcement on the BBC television evening news. Gwen stood watching from the doorway, still trembling in fear. As with the whole country, and indeed the whole of the western world, they had all been living in fear about the prospect of a nuclear world war. But Gwen in particular had been completely unable to live with this threat. She had become withdrawn within herself and had very rarely gone out of the house during this time. She had also stopped communicating with her family in any normal way. Roy had noticed this change in his wife and had been particularly concerned about it.

The news announcer explained to the nation that Khrushchev had finally agreed to remove the Soviet Union's nuclear missiles in Cuba, which everyone in the USA and around the western world knew by now were threatening the United States. He also explained that the Soviet Union had agreed never to invade Cuba without direct provocation, and that, in the interest of world peace going forward, the United States and the Soviet Union had agreed to set up a telephone hotline to allow instant communication between the two major world powers in an attempt to curtail any further dispute serious enough to threaten nuclear war and the annihilation of the people and the world as we knew it.

It had been the closest the world had come to entering into full-scale nuclear war, and a near-run thing. Roy and the children all cheered and clapped as the implications of the announcement became clear. Gwen burst into tears. Roy only realised Gwen's reaction when he turned around to beam in relief at her. He immediately went and took her in his arms.

'It's all over, darling! Nuclear war has been averted!' He found himself crying with relief and joy in her arms.

But Gwen could not be comforted in the days and weeks that followed, however much Roy tried his best to do so. He and their family, and indeed the rest of the nation and the world, resumed their normal daily lives, relieved beyond belief by the peaceful outcome of this near catastrophe for mankind. As for Gwen, she continued to move around the house morosely, frequently bursting into tears from time to time for no apparent reason.

Roy completely understood his wife's reaction to this situation, and he acknowledged that, while all of his family and the world in general had breathed a sigh of relief and gone on with their lives, for the moment Gwen was not able to do so. He recognised that this was a feature of her longstanding vulnerability to anxiety and depression, a vulnerability that she was unlikely ever to change. He couldn't help thinking back to the confident young woman, trained nurse and mother that he had first married, but in his heart he realised that her present mental agitation was a characteristic she had presumably inherited and something that they were both likely to need to navigate further together in the years to come.

He was grateful when, after a few months, Gwen too was able to recover from the frightening threat that had enveloped them all. She now resumed her normal life with no indication that she was still experiencing depressive thoughts. For the moment at least.

CHAPTER 24

Roy sat at his desk in his office looking at the letter in front of him. It was from Her Majesty's Revenue & Customs and began with the header: "Notice of Forthcoming Selective Employment Tax".

The letter went on to say that, from the sixth of April next year, all businesses would be liable to pay extra taxes for each person in their employ.

Roy's face turned ashen as he took in the details set out in the letter. He had seen a mention in the newspaper a few months before that the government of Harold Wilson was planning to introduce extra taxation on businesses from April 1966. That particular newspaper, the *Manchester Guardian*, had claimed that Wilson had come under the influence of two Hungarian-born economists, Nicholas Kaldor and Thomas Balogh, and the paper had thought the whole plan bizarre. Roy had really not taken in any of the details at the time, let alone considered that it might have a significant impact on him and his company. The newspaper had explained that the tax was intended to subsidise manufacturing industries to help exports and was designed to be a tax on companies that did not boost exports. At the time, the proposals had seemed very esoteric to Roy, and he had not understood that any of this would affect him much.

The letter in front of him now set out the details of the new tax. There was to be a weekly payroll tax of twenty-five shillings for each man on the payroll; twelve shillings and six pence for each woman employed. There were nearly eighty employees of Strange & Sons at that time – at one time there had been as many as a hundred – which would amount to his company being liable for one hundred pounds of extra taxes every week, or over five thousand pounds a year. That was a colossal amount of money for him to lose from his budget.

A percentage of the present workforce were past their statuary retirement age and, through no fault of their own, were less productive than they had been in earlier years, although Roy would not have thought for one moment about bringing this to their attention. This group included some of his most long-serving and loyal employees, such as Henry Dalloway and Hector Munn, the senior carpenter and joiner, and Munn's deputy, Ken Wright. Because of their invaluable and long-serving commitment to the company, Roy had kept many of them on the payroll because he considered he had a duty to do so, even though he was well aware that they were now less productive.

Basil Chart knocked on his door and, when Roy called 'come

in', entered with a cup of coffee in his hand and stood swaying and bobbing in front of Roy.

'Cup of coffee, sir?' he asked. Mr Chart was an older man, about fifteen years older than Roy himself. He was thin as a rake with a beaked nose, large brown horned-rimmed glasses and an Adam's apple big enough to cause you to want to stand aside and hug the corridor wall to make room as he passed. He had the habit of walking around everywhere with a battered old clipboard, to make himself look busy. He also had this peculiar habit of bobbing and swaying; when he passed you in the corridor, he would bob to the side and then sway back again after you had passed him.

He was really quite flea-bitten, with his threadbare light-brown jacket with its dark-brown scratched leather patches sewn onto both elbows and his worn green corduroy trousers. Not only was he threadbare in dress, he was also a painfully unctuous individual, sometimes exasperatingly so. Even Roy, who was normally a mild-mannered man, got quite irritated by Basil's sycophantic manner at times. He referred to Chart as "Uriah Heap" when he was at home with Gwen. "Always your humble servant" was the joke from the Dickens character that made them laugh. He may have been innocuous and faithful, but he was another employee who Roy had kept on out of loyalty, even though, in his case, he was pretty useless.

'Thank you, Basil. Please put it on the desk,' Roy said, fearing the man would spill the whole cup of coffee on the floor if it didn't reach dry land soon. Chart swayed forward, placed the cup perilously on the edge of the desk and then bobbed back upright again.

Chart noticed Roy's concerned face and said, 'Everything all right, sir?'

He was the only employee of the firm who insisted on calling Roy "sir", in spite of having been with the firm for nearly thirty years. All the other men, from Henry Dalloway down to the junior apprentices, addressed him as "guv'nor", a name he had inherited from his father Frank, the original "guv'nor" of Strange & Sons.

'Yes, thank you, Basil,' Roy replied, moving the cup of coffee carefully into the centre of the desk as he did so.

'Will that be all, sir?'

'Yes, thank you, Basil,' Roy replied wearily.

Chart bobbed out of the office, shutting the door behind him. He was the only employee he would not be sorry to lose, Roy thought to himself.

*

The next day, Roy sat in the office of his accountant in Town Hall Square. Alan Farrell was a wise opinion, who had served Roy's father Frank, and indeed Strange & Sons and himself, since he had taken charge of the company. Farrell was well aware how tight things had become for Roy in recent years. Roy had worked hard to rejuvenate the company's residential housing business since the loss of the wartime defence contracts, and his business of Strange & Sons had met with great success during the 1950s and early 1960s. But more recently, in spite of the high reputation of the family building firm, known for its excellent work and reliability, the truth was that the situation had become more difficult for the building industry locally. His main competitor, a firm called Larkins, were now doing a thriving business in the town. They had stolen a significant part of the market by building "quick and cheap" and had attracted a large clientele of customers who did not know better. But Roy had been shocked by the poor quality of many of their houses that he came across.

He had been particularly irritated recently by finding out that Larkin was erecting a number of blocks of high-rise flats on marshy land at the base of Galley Hill, to the far east end of the town's seafront. Roy had been offered the land himself a year or two back but had turned down the offer, having come to the conclusion after a detailed survey that it was not secure building land. The fact that the blocks of flats Larkin had built there had already started to develop significant settlement cracks, not to mention extensive rusting of the steel balconies and other metal structures observable from the road, appeared to justify Roy's reluctance to build there. But Larkin had sold them all on with a handsome profit by this time.

'I'm afraid you're right, Roy.' Alan Farrell agreed with his assessment. 'This new selective employment tax is going to make things even more difficult for you.'

'I'm not sure that the company can survive this in the present climate once this selective employment tax has been introduced,' Roy said. 'I anticipate the tax will be around for a good few years, at least.'

'So, what do you want to do?' Farrell asked him, sitting back in his chair and placing his pen on the desk.

'I really don't know, Alan,' Roy replied. The choices were bleak.

'Well, you've got six months to decide before the new tax comes in. And you know I shall be here to help you navigate these choppy waters, whatever you decide.'

*

Three weeks later, Roy sat down with Gwen with a cup of tea after Sunday lunch.

'I've got something important to tell you, darling,' he started. 'I'm afraid I'm going to have to close down Strange & Sons. I've decided to liquidate the company.'

'But, Roy ... *why*!' Gwen couldn't hide her alarm. 'What are we going to live on?'

Roy explained to her about the new employment tax that was going to be introduced in April. 'It would be too heavy a blow to withstand financially, in the present climate. I fear we wouldn't survive it. Instead of sitting and watching the company go bankrupt, I've decided to file for voluntary liquidation. We'll get by with Alan's help. But it is going to be a bit of struggle for a while. I want to see all our employees retired on adequate pensions and do my utmost to find suitable alternative employment for those that are too young to retire.'

Roy was as good as his word. He spent the next six months working perhaps as hard as he had ever worked, deciding what should happen to his trusted workforce.

One Monday, he called all the men into his office one by one to tell them what was going to happen. He asked them not to be alarmed, to trust him. He assured the older men who expressed the desire to retire that he would make sure they did so with an adequate pension, which they had surely earned. To the younger men who needed to carry on working, for their own and their family's sakes, he said that he was determined to find them alternative work that would be acceptable to them, both professionally and financially. To a man, they all took it calmly, expressing their trust in him and thanking him for what Strange & Sons had done for them for so many years. Roy felt humbled by their response.

The word about Strange & Sons' liquidation soon got out and spread like wildfire in the local industry. The *Bexhill Observer* did not help with its report under the emotive headline: "Local firm to finish trading". Everybody he spoke to had immediately assumed that the firm had gone "bust", and he had to explain repeatedly that no, this was not the case, but that he had decided to sell the company before rather than after he retired himself. He would add that none of his three sons were interested in taking the business over from him, although he never mentioned that he would advise them not to do so in the present climate if this were the case.

But try as Roy did to tell the real reason for his decision to close the firm, the vultures were starting to circle. Henry Dalloway reported back to him that he'd had to "see off" a number of unsavoury fellows who had wandered into the yard uninvited to see what they could pick up "on the cheap". Roy had hoped to sell the company as a going concern, but it soon became clear that this was not going to happen. His main rival Larkin had become so dominant locally – cornering such a large part of the market – that potential buyers of the company knew this and shied away from setting up in competition with him.

So Roy started the process of selling off the company's property, land and equipment piece by piece. Henry Dalloway watched in silence day after day as their equipment was loaded into other company's vans and taken away. Hector Munn, who was also retiring, and Ken Wright, his deputy joiner, were downcast as their carpenters' shop was dismantled and all their precious tools sold at auction. Albert Smith was in tears as he saw the last lorry being driven out of the yard by its new owner.

Roy too found that the business of liquidating the company that his father had built up and he had continued to run was a more difficult undertaking than he could have imagined. The whole process was physically tiring but emotionally even more so. He was strong enough to cope with this himself. But what he found most distressing was the effect that his decision to sell off the firm was having on Gwen.

She had become sad and depressed, unable to cope with the

change in their lives, and had withdrawn into herself again to the point that he was barely able to communicate with her in any meaningful way. Very occasionally he even found himself becoming cross with his wife: *why couldn't she accept the situation, as he'd had to? He'd had to find the strength to cope with all this change,* he'd said to himself. Even worse, once or twice he had found himself asking why she could not give him the support a wife was supposed to give her husband, at his greatest time of need. But as soon as any such thoughts passed his mind, he vanquished them, telling himself that becoming bitter and blaming Gwen was beneath him. He should know better.

CHAPTER 25

Roy's mother, Emma Lydia Baines, died at home on the first of April 1966. She was eighty-four. The week the new selective employment tax was coming into being, Roy thought to himself, somewhat ironically.

After his father had died, the old lady had insisted on living on her own in the bungalow Roy had built her on land next to the site of the company's overflow yard at the bottom end of Springfield Road, in the north of the town. Geoffrey, who was seventeen by now, had been doing his bit helping to look after his grandmother. He would cycle up to her place every Saturday morning and pick up the list of groceries and other things she needed. He would then cycle to the shops to pick them up for her. It was never an easy job to decipher what was on the list, his grandmother's handwriting being almost illegible at times, her frail italic script blurred by her pronounced tremor those days. But he got used to her weekly grocery and other needs, and what he could not decipher clearly from her list he got good at making an intelligent guess about. He was usually right.

'Everything all right with Granny?' Gwen asked Geoffrey one Saturday when he arrived home on his bicycle for lunch. Over the years, Gwen had got to like the old lady. She was less aloof and judgemental than she had seemed to be when Gwen had first met her and during the early years of her marriage to Roy, when she had compared her to Queen Mary. She seemed to have mellowed with time, Gwen thought to herself. Or perhaps it was just that she had become friendlier herself to the old lady as the years passed? In Emma's very old age, Gwen had become protective towards her mother-in-law, checking on her regularly to see that she was all right. She couldn't help feeling sorry for the old lady living alone on her own, but Emma had been adamant that that was how she wanted to live out her life.

'She is getting very frail, Mum,' Geoffrey said. 'And I noticed today how very thin she has become. I haven't mentioned this before, but recently she has always had a large bottle of aspirin on her shopping list. She seems to be getting though loads of it. When I asked her why she needed so much aspirin, she only gave me her little grin and a giggle and said something about it being for her tummy pain.'

'That doesn't sound too good, Geoffrey. I'm glad you mentioned it to me. I'll get your father to ask Dr Winchester to call in on her to see how she is.'

Dr Winchester did call and see Granny Baines. What he found was that she was complaining of severe upper abdominal pain, which was boring through into her back. She told him she had been getting very little sleep because of the pain recently.

'That doesn't sound too clever, my dear,' Dr Winchester said to her. 'How long has this been going on?'

'Oh, ages, doctor,' the old lady replied.

The GP helped her onto her bed. When he examined her, he found that she was grossly emaciated, her ribs sticking out from her chest and her abdomen concave. There was a mottled brown burn mark on the skin of her upper abdomen where she had fallen asleep night after night with a very hot water bottle held tightly to it, in an effort to ease the pain. When he attempted to examine her abdomen, she tensed and gave a shriek of pain at his most gentle of touches.

'I don't like the look of this, Mrs Baines,' Dr Winchester told the old lady once he had given her time to dress. 'I think you may have developed a nasty ulcer in your stomach. I am going to refer you urgently to Mr Plummer, the surgeon at the hospital, for his opinion. In the meantime, I would strongly advise you to discontinue all those aspirins Gwen tells me you have been taking.'

'I've only been taking them to help ease the pain, doctor. Geoffrey buys them for me at the chemist. He's been a great help to me recently. He comes up on his bike every Saturday morning to do my shopping for me.'

'Well don't ask him to buy any more, and flush the rest down the loo, Emma. If they're not the cause of your ulcer problem, they certainly aren't making it any better.' With that, Dr Winchester got up to leave. 'You should be receiving a letter with an appointment to be seen in the hospital clinic very shortly. I'm sure Roy will drive you there, if you let him know when it is.'

But it was too late. The old lady was found dead in bed one morning a few days later. It seemed she had been vomiting blood over her bed clothes during the night. Dr Winchester signed her death certificate. The cause of death he gave was "perforated peptic ulcer". Roy and Gwen were sad to lose the old lady. Gwen couldn't help but think back to her days at St James' and all the patients with acute peptic ulcers she had seen Mr Tanner operate on and save. She wondered if it would have made any difference if her mother-in-law's problem had come to light sooner. But she probably would have been too frail to survive major surgery by the time it came to light, she had to conclude.

CHAPTER 26

Eventually the family building firm of Strange & Sons had been sold off completely. Roy had obtained as much money as he could for the estate and all the equipment that went with it. He had used most of what he had raised in the sale to maximise the pension pots of all the long-serving employees who were retiring. He had also found satisfactory employment for every one of the fifty or so workers who still needed to work on. He had certainly done his duty.

The company had been liquidated. The Inland Revenue were still on his back and would continue to be for a year or two more. The problem was that someone in the HMRC office could not believe that he hadn't chosen voluntary liquidation to hide some illicit earnings from them somehow. They had been unable to believe that someone in Roy's position had undertaken voluntary liquidation as a wholly philanthropic move to protect his employees from unplanned redundancy. But Alan Farrell was sorting things out for him and eventually his tax affairs were satisfactorily settled. Roy was exhausted by the end of the process, which had taken about two years of his life to complete.

From the beginning, Roy had passed the story around that he was liquidating the company voluntarily prior to his own retirement as a way of getting those around him who might question his motives off his back. But when the job was finished, and the company closed, he knew that he was too young to retire himself. He was only fifty-six, after all, and still had his wife and children to support in one way or another. In any case, he had lived for his work and the company. He had to smile when he thought back to his younger self who'd had ideas of breaking away and ploughing a different furrow; how he had branched off on a completely different career in electronics for a time.

He was still grateful for the training and experience he had gained working for Pye, which had stood him in good stead later, but was nevertheless very happy that the unexpected death of his father had thrown him back into the company. Once he'd taken over the reins, he had enjoyed every minute of it and was grateful for the colleagues and friends he had acquired during all the years he had spent running the business. The work they had done as a team to erect the anti-tank sea defences all along the coast had been something he remembered with pride, but the smaller satisfactions of providing quality work and service to each of his customers, while less easy to measure, was also something he cherished.

The problem he now had to face was: what should he do

next? He hadn't lost money by winding up the company, but he hadn't made any either, after all his commitments to the workforce had been honoured. He still needed to earn a salary for himself and Gwen to live on. He started putting out feelers and answering job adverts. As soon as he did so, he realised that it was not going to be easy. Men he had known for decades in the building and related trades were polite and gave him a sympathetic hearing. But at the end of the day, they were unable to offer him a job. They shook him kindly by the hand and wished him well in whatever position he found for himself. But the weeks and months passed and Roy started to despair seriously whether he was ever going to be able to find employment again in his life.

During the time that passed while Roy was selling off the firm and looking for further employment, his eldest son Michael had gone to medical school in London and was nearing qualification as a doctor; his daughter Elizabeth had obtained a degree in education and qualified as a teacher; and his second son Geoffrey was following his older brother Michael into medical school. Only their youngest son Paul was still at school, living at home and still dependent on his parents.

Eventually, after nearly two years' hunting, a job came up that he thought would suit him adequately. The advert was for the position of deputy manager of a builders' merchant company in Uckfield, a town about twenty miles north of Bexhill. He knew it would not set his world on fire – he was far too over-qualified for the post, both in training and experience, but he played his qualifications down at the interview for the post. It was difficult enough for a man in his late fifties to find a new job, and he did not want to be turned down on the grounds that he was over-qualified. Following the interview, he was offered the job. The pay was only a fraction of what he had earned as the boss of Strange & Sons, but it would bring something in on a regular basis and pay into his pension fund until he was ready to retire completely. He accepted the job offer and started work a couple of weeks later.

Try as hard as he could to put his best effort into the new job, Roy soon became disillusioned with it. He found the twenty-mile trip by car to work and back every day quite tiring. But he could have coped with that if the job had been more stimulating. The company's owner and manager, Cliff Jones, was friendly enough. He was more than ten years younger than Roy, although he did engage with Roy on his own level. But the fact was, the nine-to-five job quickly became tedious for Roy, who had been used to running his own company and its large team of employees. He quickly became bored. But worse than the boredom was the irritation that he soon developed with the sloppy attitude and laziness of the other half a dozen younger men working in the builders' merchant. He couldn't stand that and took to telling Cliff so. Most of them would not have survived had they been working with him at Strange & Sons. But he wasn't a man to give up easily and just had to soldier on.

CHAPTER 27

'*D-E-C-I-M-A-L-I-S-ATION*,' the singer on the radio was shouting out. '*We call it decimalisation, decimalisation.*'

'Do turn that pop music down, Paul,' Gwen said to her youngest son. 'It's ever so loud!'

'It's Max Bygraves, Mum. It's his new release.'

'*Decimalisation, decimalisation*,' the singer crooned on merrily.

'What on earth was he going on about, anyway?' Gwen asked after the song had ended.

'It's all about the change to our new currency, Mum. Surely you haven't forgotten next Monday is Decimal Day, when the new money comes in?'

'Well, that's all news to me, Paul,' Gwen said, sounding quite alarmed. 'I'm sure your father would .have discussed it with me if it was so important!'

'Dad's been aware of it for years, Mum. I'm sure he must have told you about it. Anyway, you've been seeing 5p and 10p coins in your change for three years now. You must have realised what was going on? They're the same as the old one shilling and two shilling bits.'

'Well, I thought they were fake coins – I've been throwing them away in the bin whenever I saw one.'

'Oh, Mum – what a waste! Didn't you ask Dad what they were all about? Or, better still, you could have passed them on to me. I could have done with the cash. If you've got any new 50p pieces still in your handbag, I'll definitely relieve you of those – they're worth ten shillings now. Haven't you noticed that there are no ten-shilling notes in circulation now – they've all been withdrawn?'

*

Monday, the fifteenth of February 1971 – Decimal Day – dawned, but Gwen was still not expecting much change to her way of life. The banks had been closed from three thirty p.m. on Wednesday the tenth of February to ten a.m. on Decimal Day, Monday the fifteenth of February, to enable all outstanding cheques and credits in the clearing system to be processed and customers' account balances to be converted from £sd – pounds, shilling and pence – to decimal. But since Gwen had almost never written a cheque in her life – she left all the finances and money side of things to Roy – she was blissfully unaware of such matters.

The next Wednesday, Gwen walked down Terminus Avenue

to do her shopping at the International Store in Collington Mansions, at the end of their road. She went there every week, usually on a Wednesday when it was less busy than on Fridays and Saturdays. She liked the shop because she could buy everything she needed in one place; it combined groceries and vegetables with household goods. There was a helpful butcher on the meat counter and it even had a fish counter at the back of the store. So she could get all she needed for the family's meals and the house in one shop, without having to make the longer walk into the centre of town. There was also a greengrocer's shop on the pavement next door if she needed any other fresh vegetables that the International might not have in that week.

This week, as she walked around the counters of the shop, Gwen was confused to see that the prices of everything on display had changed. A bag of potatoes was now shown as "5p" with "1 shilling" listed in smaller print underneath it. In fact, for some months, the grocer had been showing all his prices as, for example, "1 shilling" with the new currency "5p" in smaller letters below it. But Gwen had ignored all these additional prices and had carried on as usual, somehow assuming that this had nothing had to do with her, as had, to be fair, a large proportion of the population – the older ones, at least.

At the end of the first week of being faced with the new currency, Gwen arrived home with her shopping and poured the contents of her purse onto the kitchen table. She stared at the foreign money and realised she had no idea what all these new coins added up to. For the first time in her life she had come home from shopping not sure what she had bought and, more importantly, how much it had all cost her. When this reality occurred to her, she broke into tears. She made herself a cup of tea and tried to pull herself together.

But when Roy came home from work that evening, he had hardly come through the front door when she burst into tears again.

'What is it, my love?' he asked, taking her in his arms. 'What's been happening today?' He assumed there must have been some accident or tragedy that she had been waiting to tell him about.

Gwen stayed in his arms, blurting out how unhappy she was. It was only after quite a few minutes that Roy understood that it was the new change to decimal currency that was upsetting her so much.

'But darling, this has been discussed for some time now,' he said, sitting her down on the sofa next to him. 'It's not as if we've not had any warning about it.'

As soon as he said this, he realised that, busy as he was, he had not had the chance to warn Gwen on Monday that the change in the money was actually going to happen that week. He had assumed, foolishly he now recognised, that she was quite prepared for the change and was ready for it. He now knew that this had been unwise of him, because he had also come to know in recent years that his wife was someone who was less able to accept change easily. Her reaction to his selling off the business had been one example of this.

Thinking over that fact, he could not help wondering why

this was. When they had first met and married, she had been a professional person, able to ride all sorts of change in her life and their lives – leaving home to train as a nurse; the changes from qualified nurse, to senior theatre sister, to district nurse; the birth of their first child; the war and evacuation to Hooe, for instance – all of which she had coped with not only as being inevitable but had actually seen the changes as exciting challenges in their lives. But now, as the years had passed, he had become aware that she was much less able to cope with life in general and change in particular. She was much more vulnerable than when he had first met and married her, and he was going to have to be more attentive and supportive, if he could, to help her cope with this vulnerability that she had acquired over the years.

As the weeks went by, Gwen carried on with her shopping largely as usual, trying to ignore the new system, which was completely opaque to her way of thinking. Roy and Paul seemed to think that all this change was progress – a good idea – so she supposed she had to live with it. But she was still unhappy by the fact that something she took as part of her normal day-to-day life – her shopping – had been disrupted in this way.

'I don't like this new halfpenny – it's much too small,' she would complain to Paul when he came home from school. 'And I can't find any sixpenny pieces anywhere! What are we going to do without our favourite tanners? Anyway, the worst thing about all this, it seems to me, is that the shops are using the whole thing as an excuse to put their prices up.'

She was not the only member of the public making this

complaint. Armies of housewives up and down the country were objecting to what they considered was a rise in the cost of living by stealth, and Roy and Paul had to agree reluctantly that things did seem to be more expensive overall these days, in spite of their support for "progress".

For several years, most of the shops Gwen used would continue to show their prices in £sd as well as pounds and new pence. But she would ignore the labels and continue to ask the patient greengrocer, 'How much is that in old money?' Gwen was only one of many of his customers who were not able to get to grips with the new currency, and he would politely convert the price back to them into £sd. He was just as polite when some of them would also ask him, 'How much is that in real money?'

The day came, however, when Gwen, with everyone else, finally had to accept that the change had occurred and she was going to have to live with it. The reminders of the conversion value of the new prices into the old currency were beginning to disappear. But she had been more upset by the change in her everyday life than most.

CHAPTER 28

Roy was very concerned about Gwen. She was in her late fifties now, but had been bleeding almost continuously for some months. She also had a constant dragging pain in her lower abdomen and pelvis, which made it difficult for her to stand and walk for any prolonged period of time. She appeared very pale to him, and he guessed she must have become quite anaemic with this continuous blood loss.

'We've got to do something about this, darling,' he said to her one evening, after he had come home from work and found her crying in pain leaning over the kitchen sink. 'I'll give Dr Winchester a ring and ask him to refer you to a gynaecologist.'

He knew that Gwen, in spite of her years of nursing experience, was reluctant to visit doctors on her own behalf and disliked making a "fuss". He rang the surgery only to find that good old Winchester had retired. Nevertheless, his younger partner Dr Wicks appeared on their front door step later on that evening.

Dr Wicks took one look at Gwen, examined her abdomen and said quietly to her: 'I agree with Roy, Mrs Baines. This needs to be sorted out. I can see how much it's dragging you down. I'll refer you to Mr Thomas at the Buchanan Hospital.'

'Oh, no,' Gwen blurted out. 'I don't want to be seen locally!'

'In that case,' Dr Wicks said, 'London it is. What about The Westminster Hospital? Michael's working there at the moment, isn't he?'

Within a matter of days, Gwen and Roy found themselves sitting on the seventh floor of The Westminster Hospital. They were in the waiting room of the private suite of the senior gynaecologist, Mr Roger de Vere. Gwen was visiting as a non-private patient – there was no way Roy and she could afford to pay Mr de Vere's full private fees – but they were being given this treatment in acknowledgement that their son Dr Michael Baines was working as a house physician in the same hospital, where he had trained.

'Do come in, Mr and Mrs Baines.' Mr de Vere appeared from his consulting room dressed in a tailcoat and purple silk waistcoat to shake their hands. 'Please make yourselves comfortable,' the gynaecologist said, pointing to the two leather chairs on the other side of his desk.

'I've had the referral letter from your GP, Dr Wicks. I understand you have been bleeding more or less non-stop for a few months now and are having quite a bit of lower tummy pain?' he asked Gwen.

'Yes, I have,' Gwen replied quietly. She was feeling rather

humiliated to find herself in this position. As a trained nurse, she had learnt not to complain about her own health problems, which had always been trivial compared to the patients she had found herself caring for. In spite of having learnt to cope with some of the *prima donna* surgeons she had worked with at St James' Balham, she still could not help feeling somewhat intimidated by being in the presence of this rather important man, sympathetic though he might have been.

'Let's have a look at you,' de Vere said. 'Hop up on the couch, my dear. I just need to feel your tummy.'

Gwen went behind the screens, undressed to her underclothes and climbed onto the couch. Mr de Vere came round the curtains and started to examine her abdomen.

'Just as I thought, my dear. You've got some prize fibroids there! Excuse me if I feel inside.'

Hardly giving her a chance to object, he proceeded to conduct an internal examination. Gwen of course knew that this was necessary and what it entailed, but again, being on the receiving end, could not help feeling foolish as she winced in surprise.

'We'll sort all this out for you, Gwendoline,' de Vere said, as soon as she had dressed and returned to her seat next to Roy. 'I'll put your name down for an urgent total hysterectomy as soon as possible. That means taking out the "box" and, at the same time, removing the ovaries. You don't need those any more, do you?'

He didn't give her time to reply. 'And it's best not to take the risk that they might become "naughty" in the future, isn't it?'

Gwen knew he was referring to cancer but did not have the energy to tell the eminent surgeon this. She wasn't even sure if he knew she was a trained nurse and did not have the strength to enlighten him if this was the case.

CHAPTER 29

Gwen was discharged from hospital only a week after her surgery. Roy drove up to London to bring her home and had been very attentive to her since she'd arrived back. The surgery had gone well and her scars were healing nicely. But that wasn't the point. Before Gwen was discharged, Mr de Vere had taken Roy aside and warned him that many of his "gals" went through a period of depression following a hysterectomy.

'It's difficult for us chaps to understand,' he had said, 'but try and put yourself in Gwen's shoes. Think what it would be like for a man to go through the same loss of parts!'

Roy had tried to nod understandingly but was shocked. The surgeon meant well, but he could not help thinking that the analogy he was using was just a little crude.

What Gwen was now having to deal with during the initial weeks and months following her "total" hysterectomy was not anything to do with a psychological reaction to the loss of her womanhood, however. More prosaically, her early symptoms were profoundly physical. Although her periods had more or less petered out a few years before – until these last few months of heavy bleeding, that is – since the removal of her ovaries she was now experiencing severe continuous hot flushes that invaded all her waking and sleeping hours. As time passed, these physical post-menopausal symptoms were overtaken by a severe change in her mood. She'd had a tendency to episodes of anxiety and depression throughout her life, which would fluctuate with times when she was a little more euphoric than usual. But now she found herself experiencing feelings of profound depression, unlike anything she had ever experienced before, and had no way of coping with this.

After Gwen had been struggling with these horrible hot flushes and severe depression for months, Roy decided to make himself an appointment to see Dr Wicks in the surgery to discuss what could be done to help her with these problems.

'Ah, yes,' Dr Wicks said to Roy when he heard about Gwen's problems. 'That will be the "surgical menopause".'

It was not the first time Roy had noticed that Dr Winchester's junior replacement had been keen to produce medical labels for any condition that he was confronted with, unlike old man Winchester, who had always been more reflective about problems that he might not have an immediate answer for. As he thought about Wicks' reply now, Roy didn't think that giving a descriptive title to consequences of the surgery Gwen had gone through helped either of them understand why she might have developed such a profound sadness since.

'I know Gwen has been prone to having low episodes during her life,' Roy stated truthfully, 'but don't you think that the present episode might be related to the sudden changes in her hormone levels she has been having to cope with since the surgery?' he asked the young doctor. 'Mr de Vere did warn me that many women do go through this problem after having had a hysterectomy, but I never imagined it might lead to such an extreme problem. If I had known this before, I might not have been so keen for Gwen to go ahead with the surgery.'

'Yes, it might well be the case that Gwen's depression has been caused by the sudden drop in her hormone levels,' Dr Wicks agreed. 'But I'm afraid there's not much we can do to treat the problem. Gwen will just have to sweat it out. The trouble does settle with time. As you know, all women do have to go through the menopause sooner or later in life. I'll give you a script for some St John's wort tablets for her to take. These often help a great deal.'

Dr Wicks had meant to be a sympathetic ear, but Roy left the surgery clutching the prescription sensing that the man had been completely out of his depth with this problem and knew he had no effective remedy for it.

Roy collected the tablets from Boots pharmacy and made sure Gwen took them regularly, as prescribed. But her hot flushes and depression showed no sign of settling down and Roy could see that the tablets were useless. After a while, he stopped insisting that Gwen should keep on with them. Gwen's hot flushes showed no sign of abating, but even worse was the fact that her severe depression was becoming more and more profound and ever more difficult for both her and Roy to cope with.

CHAPTER 30

One Saturday morning, Roy was sitting at his desk sorting out a few of the bills that had arrived recently, prior to dropping into the bank on Monday to pay them. He heard Gwen in the hall putting on her coat.

'Are you going out?' he called to her lightly from his study, where the door stood open. He felt he had to keep an eye on her these days because of her depression and the fact that he was not sure whether she was safe going out alone. He kept tabs on her movements as best he could, without wanting to make her aware that he was checking on her.

'There are a few things I need from the shops,' she called back flatly.

'Would you like me to drive you there, darling?' he asked, getting up and looking through the study door.

'I thought I'd walk down myself, now that it has stopped raining. A bit of fresh air might do me good,' she replied unconvincingly, taking two of her shopping bags off the hook in the hall.

'Take care, sweetheart,' he said, as she opened the front door and left. Roy looked out of his study window as she walked down the drive and turned left in the direction of the few local shops at the end of their road.

It was only about half a mile to the local shops, but Gwen walked slowly and aimlessly these days and it took her some time to reach there.

When she arrived at the shops, she made for the International Store, where she did a lot of her shopping these days. It saved her making a journey into the town centre. She held her two large shopping bags in one hand, using the other hand to pull the shop door open. The doorbell rang as she did so.

Gwen headed for the creamery section and started to fill one of the bags slowly with eggs, butter, milk and cheese. When she had what she needed from those shelves, she walked to the other side of the shop and continued to fill the other bag with household goods: toilet rolls, detergent and greaseproof paper, as well as a loaf of bread and tins of soup and baked beans. She stopped to think for a minute. She thought she had all that she needed that day. She'd made a list before she left home but, searching in her handbag and all her pockets, she couldn't find it now. She must have left it on the kitchen worktop.

Gwen walked slowly towards the exit. Before she reached the lady sitting at the cash till, she stopped, opened her handbag and took out her purse. Finding that it was almost empty, she snapped it closed, placed it back in her handbag and walked out of the shop, giving a sheepish smile to the lady at the cash till as she did so. She turned left towards the post office, two shops down.

Suddenly a strong hand gripped her left shoulder. Gwen spun round, alarmed, and nearly fell onto the pavement as she did so, only steadying herself by gripping the arm of her attacker with her other hand. She looked up to see the uniformed store security man staring at her.

'Please come this way, madam,' was all he said, leading her rather roughly back towards the shop front door, not removing his hand from the vice-like hold he had on her shoulder as he did so. Gwen winced in pain under the man's heavy grip but said nothing.

As they entered the store again together, at least half a dozen shoppers who had seen what was happening stood watching with open mouths as the security man marched Gwen back down the shop towards the manager's office at the back of the store.

*

Roy was still at his desk when, out of the window, he saw a police car pull up at the bottom of their drive and a policeman start walking up it towards their front door. Roy jumped up and threw the door open before the PC reached it. He looked up at the policeman, whom he recognised at once. He'd had dealings with him a few years back when the man had come to interview him after some building material and items of tools had been stolen from the firm's yard one weekend.

'Can I have a word with you, sir?' the policeman asked.

'Come in,' was all Roy replied, with no idea what this might be about. He walked the man to the kitchen, where they sat down at the table opposite each other.

'I'm sorry to inform you, sir, but we've had to arrest your wife for shoplifting at the International Store on Collington Avenue.'

'You've *what*?' Roy jumped to his feet in extreme agitation.

'I'm afraid so, sir,' the PC replied, inviting Roy to sit down again.

'This *can't* be true!' Roy continued to stand. 'My wife's a trained n-n-nurse and health visitor. She's a respectable member of the ch-ch-church.' His stammer returned with a vengeance in his distress. 'She's brought up four ch-ch-children,' he added, as a *non sequitur*.'

'I'm afraid it is, sir,' the man repeated, as sympathetically as he could, understanding Roy's distress.

'Where is Gwen? Is she all right?' Roy blurted out, sitting down suddenly at the table.

'She's in the car outside with my lady colleague,' the policeman replied. 'I thought it might be helpful if I had a few words with you before she came in.'

Leaning forward, the police constable took Roy through the events of that morning.

'We were summoned to the shop by a telephone call from the manager. The security man had made a citizen's arrest after apprehending your wife on the pavement just outside the store. He had seen her filling two of her own bags with a considerable number of items and then leaving the store with no attempt at paying for them.

'We interviewed her together with the manager in his office. Clearly, your wife was extremely upset, in floods of tears and insisting that she had had no intention of stealing the items. She claimed that she had realised that she had insufficient money to pay for the goods and was intending to return to do so once she had collected the money she needed at home.'

'Well, I'm sure that will have been the truth!' Roy almost shouted at the policeman. 'Gwen would never lie to anyone, and certainly never steal anything!'

'We did notice that your wife's... demeanour was not that of the usual type of person that we are called to arrest for shoplifting, most of whose usual reaction to being arrested is to deny any wrongdoing point blank,' the policeman acknowledged. 'Throughout our interview with your wife, she did appear unusually distracted and "down".' The man paused.

Roy bowed his head in acceptance of the situation. 'Gwen has been going through a very distressing bout of depression recently. I've been doing all I possibly can to support her through this. But it's not easy,' he added.

'We guessed the problem might be something along those lines,' the PC agreed.

'What happens now?' Roy asked with a groan.

'We discussed the situation with the store manager while

your wife waited outside the office. In view of her mental state and the fact that the address she gave us was from a respectable part of town, he agreed not to press charges. He had in any case recovered all of the goods that she had taken. She was brought back into the office, where we gave her a verbal warning. This will remain on the record, but nothing more will happen. As long as no further episodes of this nature occur in the future, of course,' the police officer added as an aside.

By this time, Roy was beginning to regain his composure, in the knowledge that the charges had been dropped against Gwen and indeed the police had had the ability to recognise and empathise with the fact that she was not well "in herself". He thanked the man as he showed him to the door to collect Gwen from the police car. The PC helped her out of the car and up the drive, passing her through to Roy and closing the door tactfully as he left.

Gwen fell into Roy's arms as she entered the hall in great distress.

'They thought I was stealing my shopping!' she sobbed. 'When I found I did not have enough money in my purse, I only meant to come home to fetch what I needed before I returned to the shop to pay for it.'

'I believe you, darling. What happened was obviously all part of an unfortunate misunderstanding.'

When she had calmed down sufficiently, he made her a cup of coffee with some brandy in it. He then took her up to their bed to sleep off the event.

Roy sat back down in his study, still significantly shaken by what had happened. He vowed then that he would accompany his wife whenever she went on shopping trips, or arrange for one of her sister's to do so if she had to go shopping while he was out at work. He knew this was committing her to a form of house arrest, which he was uncomfortable about. But he also realised that he had no alternative when she was suffering from this severe depressive illness. For the moment, at least.

CHAPTER 31

Geoffrey was busy in the kitchen of the house on Palace Road, Tulse Hill in South London, the place he rented with five other medical students in his year at medical school. He was by no means an accomplished cook, but that Saturday morning he was making a lasagne for lunch, ready for the arrival of his mother and father, who were due to pay him a visit. They had been to see one of his father's sisters in North London and were calling in to see him for lunch on their drive back down to the south coast. He had taught himself this recipe from a cookery book and had already tried it on one or two girlfriends, who had been suitably impressed. He turned the gas up high to keep the water in the pan boiling as he layered the green strips of lasagne verdi into the water and olive oil. The front door bell rang, and he hurried to open it, leaving the boiling pasta to look after itself. His father was standing there with his rather endearing sheepish grin.

'Hi, Dad, great to see you.' Geoffrey looked past his father to see that his mother was still sitting in the front passenger seat of his father's Morris Oxford car, which was parked directly outside the front gate. He followed his father down the path to greet his mother. His father opened the car door and Geoffrey bent down to kiss his mother on the cheek. In return, she barely showed any sign of recognition as she got slowly out of the car and followed him equally slowly up the path into the house.

Geoffrey sat his parents in the front room with a glass of sweet sherry each and went back to the kitchen to finish cooking the lasagne. The pasta was by now well cooked and supple, as he layered strips into the pasta dish and spooned the minced beef he had already cooked and double cream between each of several layers of pasta. He knew that the finished meal was no masterpiece but was pleased with himself that he had at least achieved some degree of cookery competence. He placed the dish of pasta onto the kitchen table and called his parents in to join him.

As they ate lunch together, Geoffrey and his father did all the talking, Geoffrey updating his parents on his final year's attachments and his father keen to hear how these were progressing and about Geoffrey's readiness for his upcoming final exams. During the whole meal, his mother hardly said a word. Indeed, she sat mutely, fiddling with the pasta on her plate without really eating much of it. Geoffrey was secretly a little disappointed with the fact that his mother had not said something to indicate that she was impressed that her son had managed to cook a meal, or even to compliment him on having achieved some basic level of competence in the culinary department.

'Well, Geoff, I suppose we must hit the road again,' his father said to him not long after they had finished lunch. 'The traffic was bad on the way here, and I don't want to have your mother arriving home too late.' That was the only brief reference his father had made to Geoffrey that his mother may not be too well, that he was having to care for her even more than he usually did.

'I understand, Dad,' Geoffrey replied, as he followed his parents back down to the car. His father opened the passenger door for his mother, who got in stiffly. It occurred to Geoffrey then that she had been moving slowly all the time during their brief visit.

His father got in to the driver's seat and leaned across his mother to wind down her window to say goodbye to him.

'Cheerio, Geoff. All the best for your final exams. We'll be thinking of you. I'm sure you're going to be fine.'

'Thanks, Dad,' Geoffrey said, as he reached across to shake his father's hand. 'I'm looking forward to finishing.'

He bent down to say goodbye to his mother. As he kissed her on the cheek, she hardly moved a muscle, apart from raising one hand very slowly in a muted farewell gesture. His father gave a breezy wave and started the engine.

Geoffrey stood on the pavement and waved as his parents' car moved off up the road. As the car disappeared round the bend, he acknowledged to himself that his mother was not well. His father had not had an opportunity to say anything about his mother to him in her presence, but Geoffrey supposed that her lack of emotional response and slowness of movement must be because she was going through another bout of her depression at the moment.

He would later process in his medical brain the fact that she had been exhibiting signs of severe clinical depression with what is known by psychiatrists as psychomotor retardation, or slowness in both the mind and the body. He hoped this would all pass very soon, as it had done in the past. But for the moment, he had a lot to think about himself. He went back into the house to clear up the lunch things before getting out his medical books to study for his exams for the rest of the weekend.

CHAPTER 32

Gwen got off the number twelve bus, which was on its way from Eastbourne to Brighton, and started to trudge up the road towards Beachy Head. She felt so oppressed by her life that, physically, she could hardly walk. She could not explain why she had been feeling so utterly depressed over the past few months. She had the sense that there was nothing occurring from outside her to cause this. No, the illness – for that is what she considered it – was coming from within her, and she had no control over it or its effect on her. It had occurred to her that her depression might in some way be a reaction to her recent hysterectomy, but she could not explain how. The disease affecting her mind and spirit was as malignant as a physical cancer, eating her away at her insides. And particularly at her mind. She and Roy had never been able to have an open discussion about how she was feeling, and she did not have the courage to talk to him about it now. She feared that he might not understand, in spite of his love for her. But she could not live like this any more. She had had enough.

She reached the top of the road and kept walking on past the Beachy Head pub until she came to the part of the cliffs she knew were the highest. There were no fences or barbed wire there. There were notices on fence posts at intervals warning of the danger. But she ignored these and walked right up to the edge of the cliff. She knew that the cliff face below was completely sheer, with no ledges or projections of any kind between the top of the cliff and the sea and rocks far below at the bottom. The wind was blowing off the sea straight into her face. She stood at the edge of the cliff not looking down but looking out at the skidding clouds, her thinning grey hair being blown around her head by the buffeting winds, tears rolling down her cheeks.

'Can I help you, my dear?' a quiet voice whispered in her right ear. She turned to see a man in a long dark raincoat, his white dog collar visible just above the open coat.

'I can't... I can't do it!' Gwen blurted out, hurling herself towards the man. As she fell into his opened coat, the Beachy Head chaplain closed his arms around her.

'It's all over,' he murmured, as he held Gwen close. 'The Lord God has heard you and has replied. You are safe in His hands now.'

*

Roy had decided for once to take a long lunch break and told his manager Cliff that he had some important matters to see to. When he arrived home, he found the house empty and his wife gone. It was not like Gwen to leave the house without telling him. The front door was unlocked, and the back door and some of the windows were wide open, which was also unlike his wife; she had always been so good about looking after the house and would never usually go out and leave the place like this.

He sat down on the chair in the hall and started thinking. As he did so, a feeling of intense foreboding came over him. Slowly, he picked up the telephone, which was sitting on the hall table in front of him, and started to call their friends. He spoke one by one to most of their closest church friends.

'Hello, Daphne,' he said. 'Excuse me calling, but I just wondered whether Gwen might have popped in to see you this morning? It's just that I've come home for lunch and she's nowhere to be seen. It's unlike her to go out for the day and forget to tell me what her plans were.'

'I'm sorry, Roy. Arthur and I have not seen Gwen since we talked to her on the church steps after the service last Sunday morning.' There was a pause. 'I have to say, we both agreed on our way home that she had not seemed herself. She was very subdued, even depressed, we thought. Not like her normal extrovert self. I do hope she is all right. If there is anything we can do to help, please let us know. It's probably a simple mistake on her part not to let you know she was going out for the day. Are you sure she isn't at the Red Cross centre, helping out there? Please, do let us know that she's all right when she comes back. Do take care, Roy.'

Roy called the Red Cross centre next, as Daphne had

suggested, and at least a dozen others of their friends. But all gave a reply to his enquiry in the negative. No-one had seen Gwen that day. More than one of the people he phoned also mentioned that she had not been looking "well" recently and wished him all the best after reassuring him that they were sure there must be a simple explanation for Gwen's absence. The more people he telephoned, the more replies he received along these lines, the more Roy started to worry about his wife. So much so that he sat by the phone without bothering to prepare himself a sandwich or eat any lunch.

At the end of his scheduled lunch break, Roy phoned his boss and told him he had matters to deal with at home and would not be coming back to the builders' merchant that afternoon.

*

Halfway through the afternoon, Roy was still sitting in the front room, staring into space, by now desperately worried about Gwen's whereabouts and her well-being. At that moment, he saw a police car pull up outside. A police officer got out and walked up the drive, knocking on the front door. Roy jumped up agitatedly and hurried to open the door.

'I'm PC Barnes,' the officer introduced himself. 'May I come in, sir?'

'Of course,' Roy replied, throwing the door open and instinctively leading the man through to the sitting room.

'Do sit down,' Roy said to the police officer. 'Is it about my wife Gwen?'

'It is, sir,' the policeman replied. Slowly but kindly, the PC proceeded to tell Roy how Gwen had been seen in a distressed state walking close to the edge of Beachy Head cliffs and how she had been approached by the Beachy Head chaplain.

'Is she... is she all right?' Roy blurted out.

'She's in the car with one of my female colleagues who has been looking after her. She's come to no harm... physically,' he added. 'We just wanted to give you a moment to prepare yourself before we brought her into the house, to give you time to hear what has been happening.'

So saying, the police officer got to his feet and waved out of the sitting room window, beckoning his colleague to bring Gwen into the house. She walked very slowly up the path to the front door, the female PC supporting her on one elbow in case she was going to fall.

CHAPTER 33

Gwen was inconsolable that evening and throughout the night that followed. Try as he could, Roy could not calm her down. She pushed him away whenever he attempted to put his arms around her and comfort her. He sat for what seemed like hours, asking her what was wrong and pleading to know what he could do to help. But he never got a reply from Gwen, at least not one that he could comprehend. She just sat there sobbing into her handkerchief, her hands shaking and her words unintelligible to him. He failed to pick up a word, let alone a phrase or sentence, that would give him a clue to what it was that was distressing her so much, enough to cause her to go wandering on her own above Beachy Head. He couldn't believe that she had been so down that she had been contemplating taking her own life, as the police officer who brought her back home had suggested. At the same time, in the state of distress she was in, he knew he could not just dismiss this as a possibility.

After about two hours' sitting with his wife and listening to her wails of distress, Roy decided that they could not go on all night like this, that he needed to call for help. He thought about who he should call. He knew he could not call her sister Freda – she was not strong enough emotionally to cope with anything like this herself. He thought about phoning the Congregational church minister, but had a sense that Gwen would have resisted this strongly if he suggested this. He knew she would not have wanted what had happened that day to be allowed to get out to any of her friends in the church, however well-meaning and understanding they might be on learning of her distress. He knew instinctively that she would be mortified with shame if the news were to spread to anyone she knew; she would not have been able to cope with what she would see as the humiliation of that.

Finally, after about three hours and as the clock struck ten, Roy decided that it was too late at night to be calling anyone. He gave Gwen a cup of Horlicks with a large measure of whisky in it and helped her up the stairs, tucking her into bed and kissing her goodnight. He went back down to the sitting room, where he sat with the door open listening to her weeping and cries of lament. He could barely bear to sit downstairs listening to his wife in such distress, but he did not know what else to do, how else to help her. After a long time, her crying settled to intermittent sobs of grief. Eventually, he could hear that these had also ceased. He went quietly upstairs and looked into their bedroom. When he had satisfied himself that Gwen was asleep and was breathing deeply, he undressed and got into bed quietly beside her, not wanting to disturb her.

The next morning Roy woke up late. He put out his arm to touch Gwen, only to find that she was no longer in the bed beside him. He jumped out of bed and pulled on his clothes hurriedly, realising he was late for work. He only had time to throw some water on his face and decided not to take the trouble to shave, which was quite unlike him.

When he came downstairs, he found Gwen in her housecoat in the kitchen. She was standing at the stove heating some water for his coffee. She turned to look at him. Her eyes were red around the rims and her hair was unbrushed, but at least her eyes were dry. She was no longer crying. She picked up the boiling kettle and as she turned to pour the water into his coffee cup, gave him a weak, sad smile.

'I'm sorry, Roy. I didn't mean to alarm you. Thank you for being so kind. I shall be all right.'

She put a plate of toast on the table and placed the cup of coffee next to it. He sat down looking at the breakfast, but didn't know what to say. He buttered a piece of toast distractedly and took a sip of coffee. Roy had never been a demonstrative man, and at this moment decided it was better to say nothing. He was not at all sure that Gwen would be "all right", but at the same time did not want to upset her again by calling any of their friends or family in to help with this crisis.

When he had finished as much of his toast and coffee as he could, Roy got up and placed the plate and cup in the sink. He turned and put his arms around Gwen. This time she didn't resist.

'Do you want to talk about it now?' he asked, whispering into her ear.

'Not at the moment, darling,' she replied. 'Perhaps later,' she said, pulling away from him. 'You'll be late for work, my love. You'd better hurry. I'll be all right now.'

Roy bent down and kissed his wife. 'If you think so,' he said, not wanting to re-open any wounds that morning. 'Promise you will call me at once if you need me, and I'll come straight home to be with you.'

Gwen nodded and smiled uneasily at him. He bent down to kiss her, picked up his car keys and left for work.

CHAPTER 34

From that day on, Roy's relationship with Gwen changed. She was still his wife, the woman he loved dearly. But he realised that he now had to start to look after her in a different, more important, way than any he had been required to do before. In practice, he became her carer. This didn't mean that he would not go out and leave her in the house alone – he had to go to work every day and couldn't avoid that. But the job he had taken on was very much nine to five and he did not have to work at the weekends. So when he was at work on a weekday, he took to phoning her a number of times a day and at irregular intervals, giving her as much verbal support with day-to-day issues as he could and reassuring himself with each call that she was coping.

It wasn't easy to judge whether she was all right at the end of a telephone, of course. Gwen had always been good at covering up her anxieties and deepest concerns ever since he had known her and long before this terrible depression had come over her. So each time he put the phone down having spoken to her from work, he would ask himself whether her replies to his questions indicated that she was really as happy as her tone on the phone had indicated.

He guessed that Gwen must have realised he was checking up on her. She must have done. During their previous married life he had never phoned her so often during the working day to check that she was all right, not even during the war years, when he had cause to be worried about her safety for other reasons. He didn't want her to think that he had taken to controlling her life. But now that he had experienced the fright of the day she went missing on Beachy Head and had realised the severity of her depressive illness, he had no choice but to keep a very close check on her.

A day did not go by after the Beachy Head incident when Gwen was not anxious and disturbed. But it was the nights that Roy found so painful to endure. He would wake regularly during the night to find that she was lying sweating next to him, half-asleep, half-awake, in a state of constant anxiety. During these times, he did not want to wake her from any sleep she might go on to have, but at the same time he would lie awake himself fretting about what he could do to help Gwen out of her state of severe anxiety and depression and guide her towards a more tranquil shore.

Throughout these fractured nights, Gwen would spend much of the time talking in her sleep, most of the time in words and phrases that he was completely unable to decipher. One night, however, she raised herself up on one shoulder, glazed but apparently fully awake, and said to him, 'It must have been horrible!'

'What, my darling? What must have been horrible?'

'Cissie's death. It must have been a horrible death.'

'What do you mean, sweetheart?'

'To be burnt to death in your nightdress while ironing. That must have been such a horrible way for a girl to die!'

'Are you awake?' He shook her gently to be certain that she was.

'It's all right, my love. It's only a dream.'

As he had done many times before, he did his best to console her from whatever this new dream had been about until, at last, she sobbed herself asleep, which allowed him to fall back to sleep again himself for a short time before he had to get up and ready for work.

It was only later that day at work that Roy realised Gwen had been referring to the death of her older sister Cissie, who she had never known. She had told him about this terrible family tragedy shortly after he had first got to know her, but it had never been referred to since. The fact that Gwen was still having thoughts about death, albeit that of her unknown sister, started to give him renewed anxiety about her parlous state of mental health and caused him to be increasingly depressed himself about her future and that of them both.

During this time, Roy was also worried by the fact that he was now working twenty miles away from home by car. If another emergency were to arrive, it would take him a while to leave work and drive down to be with her. It also meant that he could not drop in casually unannounced to see how she was coping, during his lunch hour for instance. He worked too far away to be able to drive home on his lunch break and be back in time to start his afternoon's work at two o'clock. He decided he had to make another arrangement to help him deal with this problem.

Roy telephoned Freda and asked if she could drop round for a word with him some time. She agreed immediately, without knowing why he wanted to see her, and they arranged to meet for coffee at West Winds at eleven o'clock that Saturday morning. Roy chose the day and time because he knew that Gwen had agreed to help out at the Red Cross jumble sale that morning and would not be at home. Like many other things in life, she had lost interest in her volunteer work at the Red Cross centre, which she had previously enjoyed – in spite of the tiresomeness of the supervisor Madge – and had stopped going on a regular basis. But one of the ladies she had been quite friendly with had phoned her out of the blue and encouraged her to come along to help with the jumble sale that Saturday. She told Gwen they needed all the help they could get, and Gwen had agreed.

'Thank you for coming, Freda. One sugar is what you take?' he said, putting a spoonful in the cup of coffee and handing it to her.

'Not at all, Roy. You know you can call on me at any time,' Freda said. 'What can I do to help?'

162

'It's Gwen, Freda. She's not been her... herself recently. In fact she's been generally really rather down.'

Roy did not want to be unfaithful to his wife, speaking to Freda like this without her knowledge, and certainly did not want to discuss the details of Gwen's recent "breakdown" or to tell her about the episode when she had gone missing to Beachy Head. But Freda was not a nosey woman; she was a simple woman with no malice in her and certainly would not be one to ask embarrassing questions.

'I thought Gwen had not been herself recently,' was all Freda said. 'What have you in mind, Roy?'

'I wondered if you could start spending some regular time with Gwen, visiting the house again perhaps three or four days a week while I am out at work? Like you used to do when you were helping out with the house and children when they were here. It would be a great reassurance to me, and a help to Gwen,' he added. 'Naturally, I'd be happy to give you payment for your time, just like I used to.'

'I'd be delighted to help, Roy. I understand Gwen's problems must have been a great worry to you. It will be a pleasure to give any time I can to support my younger sister. And I certainly do not want you to pay me for my visits! This is different from the time when I was being employed as a home help and nanny. We are a family, aren't we, and that's what families are for, aren't they?'

'Thank you so much, Freda. I can't tell you what a reassurance it will be for me having you here while I'm at work.

And I know that if anybody can cheer Gwen up, you will.'

So when Gwen got home from the Red Cross jumble sale that afternoon, Roy told her what he had arranged with Freda. He didn't give her a chance to object.

'It will be a great help for me and you to have her here while you are under the weather. And don't worry, I haven't told her any of the details about what's been happening to you.'

He knew Gwen remained ashamed about the Beachy Head incident and he did not want her to feel more ashamed and even humiliated by thinking that he had discussed the details with Freda.

From then on, Freda started to visit West Winds regularly on weekdays, as Roy had asked her to. Although none of them could know it at the time, it would be the last time Freda was called upon to help out with the family. Freda was to die the next year. She started to complain of a painless droop of her left upper eyelid. Her eye started to swell and the left side of her face to contort. Being a stoical woman who had, on reflection, probably never visited a doctor before in her life, she did not find the courage to see her GP until it was much too late. From him she was despatched urgently to the eye department at the Royal East Sussex Hospital in Hastings, where she was diagnosed with an incurable cancer of her left tear duct. She was admitted to hospital there and underwent surgery – complete enucleation (removal) of her left eye – followed by radiotherapy, but died very soon after. A very distressing and, at the time, a rather poignant and poetic death for an unmarried woman who had never herself had the chance to live a "full" life in most of the usual senses of the word.

But, as it turned out, Gwen would not be around to reciprocate her support for her older sister in her final days either.

CHAPTER 35

Gwendoline closed the front door quietly behind her, even though there was no-one else there in the empty house to hear her go. It was a Thursday, the one day in the week that Freda did not come to keep her company. She walked down the road, turned left under the railway bridge and then right along Cooden Drive.

In spite of it being the beginning of April, on this morning the air was warm and still. The mile-long walk out of town was hard going for her. Her brown walking shoes had been worn down over many years, the heels in need of repair, and her feet began to ache early on during the walk along the long, hard pavement. Her father would never have allowed her to wear shoes that had got into this state of disrepair, she thought to herself. But she trudged on, indifferent to the pain in her feet that the shoes were causing her. A short, overweight, older, grey-haired woman in a worn-out grey raincoat and worn-out shoes.

At the end of the long wide road, which ran parallel with the seashore – although she could not see the sea because of houses in the way – she came to the small circle in the road in front of the Cooden Beach Hotel. She ignored the wide vista of the sea that now came into view to her left. If she had cared to look out towards the beach at that moment, she would have seen the remains of a number of broken-down concrete blocks her husband's firm had been responsible for building during the war, their rusting reinforced steel rods sticking out dangerously from the crumbling concrete. But she did not care to look that way. Instead, she turned right past the war memorial and walked the hundred yards up to Cooden Beach station. She had been fighting another, more recent, personal war, and she knew she had lost it.

She pushed against the wooden doors of the station entrance and walked up to the ticket office desk. She asked the man behind the counter in a quiet voice for a single ticket to Victoria station, London, and handed over a pound note. The man barely looked up from his desk, concentrating as he was on that day's edition of the *Sporting Life*, opened at the page with the list of runners and riders for the afternoon's card at Plumpton Racecourse. He hardly noticed her face but did mention afterwards that the lady had seemed rather "distracted". He never mentioned to anyone the fact that she had taken the ticket but had left all her change on the counter, which he had quickly pocketed for himself.

When the Victoria train arrived, Gwen got into a carriage in the middle of the train and sat by herself, looking vacantly into the distance. There weren't many other passengers on the train: a number of mothers with young children, alone or in groups, going shopping or out for the day together. It was the middle of the day and there were no commuters travelling to and from work at this time. As they arrived at Haywards Heath station, a few passengers got off and a few more got on, but Gwen noticed none of this.

As the train left Haywards Heath station, Gwen got up and walked to the end of the carriage, pulled open the door and walked through into the space where the doors to get on and off the train was situated. She stood there, both hands gripping the right-hand carriage door handle hard, her eyes tight shut and her arms trembling. The train picked up pace, accelerating to its top speed towards the Balcombe tunnel, as she knew from her recent trips to survey the journey it always did. She sensed the change in sound as the train entered the tunnel, opened her eyes fleetingly to confirm that this was the case, and then screwed her eyes tight shut again against the smoky blackness of the tunnel that was now rushing past outside. She started to count slowly to fifteen seconds, which she had previously calculated was the time it took for the train to reach its top speed at the centre point of the long tunnel under the Sussex Downs.

There was a loud bang as the door flew open and Gwen was dragged out into the soot-black space of the tunnel. As the train sped out of the tunnel at the other side, the door slammed back shut again, causing one or two of the passengers in that part of the train to wonder what the two alarmingly loud bangs had been caused by. But nobody got up to investigate.

When the train stopped next at Gatwick Airport station, one of the platform assistants noticed that a door window was fully open and the door not securely shut. He opened the door, threw the window up and slammed the door shut properly, before blowing his whistle for the train to proceed. The whole incident seemed unremarkable to the man at the time, but subsequently was to become registered as one of many instances that would lead to the demise of slam-door carriages over the whole of Southern railways.

CHAPTER 36

Geoffrey was standing at the end of the bed, listening to the consultant surgeon talking to the patient who was about to undergo an emergency laparotomy for likely cancer. This was his last clinical attachment as a medical student, that of final year surgery at St Stephen's Hospital on Fulham Road. In six weeks' time he would be sitting his final medical exams and, all being well, would be looking forward to a short holiday break before starting his first post as a qualified doctor and a house physician at the Westminster Hospital.

The surgical department secretary, Joan, came hurrying down the centre of the ward to speak to the surgeon, Mr Wastell.

'There's an urgent telephone call for Baines in the office, Sir,' she said.

'Very well, Baines, you may go and answer it,' the surgeon said to him, somewhat reluctantly, having been interrupted in full flow.

Geoffrey hurried down the ward after the secretary and into

the office. She indicated the telephone receiver lying on the desk, then left, shutting the door behind her.

'Yes?' he asked tentatively into the receiver.

'Is that Mr Geoffrey Baines?' the question came from the other end of the line.

'It is. Who am I speaking to?'

'This is Sergeant McNally, Haywards Heath Police Station.'

'How can I help you?' Geoffrey said, bemused by this interruption.

There was a brief pause at the other end of the line.

'I'm very sorry to bring you this news, sir. But your mother's been found dead, and we need someone to provide formal identification of her body. Your father's been told the news but is understandably not in a fit state at present. We have been unable to contact your older brother Michael, who I have been told is a doctor. I understand you are just about to qualify yourself.'

'My god!' Geoffrey cried. 'How did this happen?'

'I think it might be easier to explain the circumstances in person,' the police sergeant said, as tactfully as he could. 'Would you be able to come down to Haywards Heath Police Station to assist us?'

Geoffrey did not have to consider his reply. 'Of course, of course, if it will help you. I'll get the first train down from Victoria that I can.'

'Thank you very much, sir. One of our officers will be waiting for you in a car at the station to pick you up. I am sorry to have had to break this news to you on the phone.'

Geoffrey placed the receiver slowly back on the phone, paused for a few moments to compose himself, then turned and took his coat from the back of the office door and left the hospital without telling anyone where he was going and why.

CHAPTER 37

Geoffrey hurried out of the station at Haywards Heath. A marked police panda car was parked on the concourse, its bodywork painted with large panels of light blue and white. As he walked towards it, the police officer standing next to the car came forward to shake his hand.

'Mr Baines? I'm PC Green. Thank you for coming down to assist. I'm sorry we have to meet under these circumstances.'

They got into the car together and the police constable drove him in silence straight to Haywards Heath Police Station. Geoffrey was still too stunned by the news to start asking the PC questions in the car.

On arrival at the police station, he was taken straight into a room behind the reception hall. A police sergeant was standing behind the desk there.

'Mr Baines? I'm Sergeant McNally. We spoke on the phone. Thank you for coming down and I'm sorry we have to meet in what must be very distressing circumstances for you.' He shook

Geoffrey's hand across the desk.

The next thing that happened was that Sergeant McNally bent down and brought up a pair of shoes from behind the desk, which he placed on the counter.

'Do you recognise these as your mother's shoes?' he asked Geoffrey directly.

Geoffrey stared at the shoes. They were a pair of lady's walking shoes, badly worn and down at the heel. He picked them up off the counter to inspect them more clearly. Turning the shoes over, he could just read the faded name of the makers stamped on the insole of the left heel: Freeman, Hardy & Willis. He also saw that there was what looked like a black burn mark along the outside of the right shoe, presumably caused, he was later to reflect, by the high voltage electric line onto which his mother had fallen. He didn't know what to say.

'I... can't be sure. I... I suppose they might be,' was all he could honestly say.

'I understand, sir. These things are not easy to take in at a time like this. PC Green, would you get the gentleman a cup of tea please.'

Once he was seated with a mug of tea in his hand, the police sergeant told Geoffrey what had happened. A platelayer walking through the mainline train tunnel at Balcombe early that morning had found a woman's body lying in the dark between the tracks. The body had fallen onto the high voltage power rail carried along the ground next to the tracks, presumably having fallen from a passing train. There were electrocution marks on her body, which may also have been hit by one or more trains passing under the tunnel as it lay there. Once the trains had been stopped in both directions and the power turned off, the body had been brought out on a stretcher with a police surgeon in attendance. He had already certified the woman as dead at the scene. Her handbag had been found on the tracks nearby her body and they had identified the woman as Geoffrey's mother from papers with her name and address on them.

'I'm sorry to have to tell you this, sir, but we think your mother's death may not have been accidental. We think she might have thrown herself off the train in the Balcombe tunnel. The driver was interviewed at Victoria station and said that he had heard two loud bangs while passing through the tunnel, but could find no reason to explain these at the time or any need to stop the train. In retrospect, these bangs were probably caused by the train door flying open and then back again as the train exited the tunnel. A platform assistant at Gatwick Airport, the first stop after Haywards Heath, remembered finding one of the train's door's windows fully open and the door not securely closed, but again did not find anything else untoward.'

Geoffrey sat and took all this in as the sergeant spoke to him. He knew he had reason not to be completely surprised by what he was hearing, but wished that this was not the case.

'Your mother's body has been taken to the mortuary at Cuckfield Hospital. Would you be kind enough to assist us by making formal identification?'

Geoffrey nodded silently and followed the two policemen back out to the panda car.

CHAPTER 38

The mortuary was round the back of the hospital, to one side of the grounds. The double doors to the mortuary were thrown open and Geoffrey stood at the threshold surveying the scene in front of him. He was familiar with such a sight, having spent hours in the dissecting room as a pre-clinical medical student as well as attending coroners' post-mortems during his clinical training.

But in the centre of the room there was only one body in this cottage hospital mortuary. It was that of a short, well-built woman, lying on the stainless-steel table. He took a few steps towards the table and, as the mortuary attendant reverently drew the white sheet back from the head and neck, he saw at once that these were indeed the features of his own mother. Her skin was waxen and as white as the sheet that had been covering it. The contours of her face were if anything made more well-defined by the statuesque stillness of it, accentuating her rather sharp-angled Roman nose. Her features were, however, set in stone, with none of the moving parts that were present in life. He later remembered noticing that, whatever terrible injuries her body may have sustained, her face appeared to be completely unscathed. There was not a single scratch visible on it.

He leant forward and kissed his mother on her cold waxy forehead.

'I love you, Mum. I always will,' was all he said.

In a flash of the boy he had only recently been, he experienced a brief flicker of surprise and disappointment that she did not reply. But then it was over. He stepped back and looked round to see the police sergeant also present, standing next to the mortuary attendant.

'Is this your mother, sir?' the sergeant asked him. 'Mrs Gwendoline Mary Baines?'

'Yes, officer, I'm afraid it is,' was all he could reply.

It sounded like a pathetic understatement at the time, and continued to be an exchange that was to haunt him for a long time to come.

CHAPTER 39

The inquest into the death of Gwendoline Mary Baines took place about three weeks after her death. The police had of course interviewed the driver and guard of the train from which she had fallen, as well as the platform assistant at Gatwick Airport, the first station the train stopped at after it had passed through the Balcombe tunnel. They had also managed to trace a number of passengers who had been on the train that day. A few of them had been aware of two loud bangs that had occurred while the train was in the tunnel – which had been caused by the door flying open and then slamming shut again as it exited – but none of them had known what the noises had been caused by at the time, or thought it necessary to report what they had heard. Nobody who was interviewed could remember seeing a woman who fitted the description of Gwen they were given. The coroner had felt it necessary to call only a few witnesses to the inquest. One of these was the police officer who had brought Gwen back from Beachy Head, when she had been found by the chaplain at the edge of the cliffs in a highly distressed state, a few weeks before she died.

Michael and Geoffrey sat either side of their father Roy in the relatives' seats on the front row of the coroner's court. Their sister Elizabeth and some of Roy's friends from the church were in the row behind. Michael had offered to speak on the family's behalf if called and Roy had accepted his offer without hesitation. When the time came, Michael stepped into the witness box and took the oath.

'You are Doctor Michael Baines, the eldest son of Mrs Gwendoline Baines, and you are also a registered medical practitioner?' was the first question the coroner put to him.

'I am, sir,' Michael replied.

'And I understand you are speaking on behalf of your father and the rest of the family?'

'That is correct, sir.'

'In which case, Doctor Baines, could you tell the court whether your mother had any previous history of mental illness, sufficient to suggest that she might have been at risk of taking her own life?'

'She had not had a formal diagnosis of depressive illness or any other psychiatric condition that might have put her at risk of self-harm, as far as I am aware, sir.'

'Were you aware of the incident a few weeks before her death when she had been rescued by the Beachy Head chaplain in a very distressed state standing at the edge of the cliffs?'

'I only learnt about the incident after her death, sir. My father has told me that he had been extremely concerned about the episode at the time, of course, and had done his utmost to support my mother and help her recover from it. I know that he had no idea that the crisis would recur or that my mother was at continuing risk of self-harm. I am certain that he would have sought help from her GP if he had considered that this was a possibility. But since he had not considered this possibility, I believe he felt it was kinder to my mother not to discuss the matter further.'

'And when you say that your mother had no "formal diagnosis" of depressive illness, Doctor Baines, did you have any reason yourself prior to her death to think that your mother may have been suffering from depression?'

Michael paused before he answered.

'In retrospect, sir, it is now clear both to myself and my brother Geoffrey that our mother had been suffering from severe clinical depression for some months before her death.'

At that instant, Michael heard a stifled moan coming from his father in the front row of the court. It was such a brief, suppressed, almost silent expression of grief that the coroner did not appear to have heard it. Or, if he did, he had tactfully shown no sign of having done so.

'But neither of us were living at home during that time,' Michael went on, 'and, as family members rather than medical professionals, that possibility was the furthest from our thoughts than it could be. We have both been as devastated by the tragic loss of our mother as has the rest of the family, including of course our father.'

'Thank you, Doctor Baines,' the coroner said. 'And finally, I understand there was no evidence that your mother had left a written note before her death. Had she expressed any prior feelings of wanting to take her own life to your father or any other members of the family?'

'No, sir, she hadn't. That is a reason why her death has been so unexpected and tragic for us all. If we had had some warning of the possibility that she might be contemplating taking her own life, we would have taken action to seek immediate and urgent support for her. The fact that we did not have such a warning or idea of the impending tragedy is something I know will haunt us all for the rest of our lives.'

The coroner paused, looking over his glasses with sympathy in the direction of Roy and his family and friends. Then he said, 'Thank you, Doctor Baines. You may step down.'

After a further pause, the coroner addressed the court. He said that he was truly sorry for Roy and his family, for the tragic loss of their wife and mother. He hoped that, with time, they would be able to find a way to get over this tragedy. He then said that he had reached the conclusion that Mrs Gwendoline Mary Baines had "taken her own life while the balance of her mind was disturbed" and that there was nothing in the evidence he had heard to persuade him that this had not been the case. His verdict was suicide, in the public perception of what his verdict meant. There was silence in the court and then, after a respectful pause, the members of the public and the press who had been present started to leave.

Roy left the courtroom last, utterly distraught, his face in his hands. Michael and Geoffrey walked beside him, both looking very sombre in their dark suits. Geoffrey could not remember having learnt in his training whether severely depressed people who might be contemplating their own self-destruction felt any guilt about how their actions might affect the lives of those they left behind. He remembered clearly the last time he had seen his mother, during his parents' visit to see him in his student digs in Tulse Hill. He could not imagine that, in the state his mother had been then, she had had the ability to "converse" with herself about the effect any actions she might take would have on others. He could only conclude in his sadness that she must have been taken over by some wicked automaton, which was the illness that had invaded her whole being. He hoped that that had remained the case right up until her end, that her rational consciousness had not returned to haunt her.

Geoffrey did not at that time or after feel any "blame" towards his mother for what had happened – she was no more to blame for her condition than any of his patients dying from cancer or any other terminal illness were to blame for their illness – and in that sense he hoped that she had not experienced guilt either. But it was plain to him that the "guilt" of her actions had now been transferred to his father. Roy was consumed with guilt as a result of the confirmation of the fact that his wife Gwen had taken her own life. He was already blaming himself for not having appreciated the severity of Gwen's depressive illness and for not taking any action to seek help for her. Geoffrey guessed his father would continue to bear that guilt, like a stone weighing heavily on him, for the rest of his life.

CHAPTER 40

It was the end of April. It had been, as the poet Eliot had said, truly the cruellest of months. Geoffrey stood at the bedroom window of his parents' empty, lonely house, staring out at the scene in front of him with a feeling of bleak hopelessness. His brother Michael had had to return to work at the hospital and his sister Elizabeth was back to teaching at her school. Some friends had taken his father and his younger brother Paul to stay with them for a few days after the inquest. He was now the only one left in the house.

Out of the window he could see the spring rain falling lightly over the garden. The dull roots of winter were indeed being stirred from the dead land by the life-giving water. He could see around the borders the lilacs and other spring flowers starting to show their heads cautiously above the parapet of winter. It should have been a time of desire for all men, but all he could feel at the onset of this spring was the weight of memory. Memories of past happiness that now carried with them the heaviest weight of all, a new and unbearable sadness.

With every tick of the old grandfather clock in the hall, this weight of sadness bore down on him with a heaviness that seemed to him too awful to sustain.

ACKNOWLEDGEMENTS

The description of the surgeon Mr Norman Cecil Tanner has been taken in part from an article published in Number 38 of the *Journal of the Association of Surgeons of Great Britain and Ireland*, December 2012, written by his son, surgeon Mr Brent Tanner, about his father.

With many thanks to my editor Vicky Richards for her professional expertise and patience with me, her co-editor Lydia Jennings and to Kirsty Jackson and all her team at Cranthorpe Millner.

ABOUT THE AUTHOR

Author's photo by Michelle Fowler

Author Jeremy Bending spent his life as a hospital doctor and consultant physician. During that time he wrote fiction and short stories, some of which were brought together in his book *A Listening Doctor*, published in 2018. Following a life-long passion for writing, after hanging up his stethoscope he embarked on a new career as a writer of fiction.

His first novel, *In the Shadows of the Birch Trees*, published in 2020, tells the story of a young Hungarian woman and her baby, following their escape from entering the Birkenau concentration camp in WW2.

If You Don't Know..., his second novel, was published in 2023, and was chosen as a finalist in the International Page Turner Writing Awards 2022. This complex thriller unravels the events surrounding the death of a diplomat, who is murdered by a Hungarian gang he uncovers trafficking Roma girls into the sex trade.

His third novel, *Impulses*, published in 2023, is the intriguing story of how a man could lose control of his basic impulses. He must be ill, but what sort of affliction could lead to such a serious change in his personality?